MISTS OF REMEMBRANCE

When she woke up in hospital the name 'Carol Legat' was on her name tag, and although it didn't sound right she accepted it. She began a new life with a man who wanted to help her trace her past. But she wanted to forget. Gradually, the nightmare she had shut out of her mind caught up with her, and then there was only one thing to do: confront it, with the help of the man who loved her.

BETTY O'ROURKE

◆

MISTS OF REMEMBRANCE

Complete and Unabridged

LINFORD
Leicester

First published in Great Britain in 1989 by
Robert Hale Limited
London

First Linford Edition
published January 1992
by arrangement with
Robet Hale Limited
London

British Library CIP Data

O'Rourke, Betty
 Mists of remembrance. — Large print ed. —
 Linford romance library
 I. Title
 823.914 [F]

 ISBN 0–7089–7135–0

Published by
F. A. Thorpe (Publishing) Ltd.
Anstey, Leicestershire

Set by Words & Graphics Ltd.
Anstey, Leicestershire
Printed and bound in Great Britain by
T. J. Press (Padstow) Ltd., Padstow, Cornwall

1

"SHE'S beginning to come round — keep an eye on her Nurse, and let me know when she's fully conscious."

The girl in the hospital bed heard the words but they made little sense to her sluggish brain. All she wanted was to lie still, drifting between sleep and waking; cocooned in her own little world.

It was some time later, when she was more fully awake, that she heard the voices again.

"What's this one's name?"

"We don't know. She was brought in from Casualty. Road accident. No identification."

"There's her handbag."

"That's no help. There's nothing much in it."

"Look, she's stirring. Ask her. I need it to complete her records."

A face peered closely into the girl's own. A cheerful voice said briskly, "Hallo, dear! Come back to join the land of the living, have you? Can you tell us your name?"

"Name?" The girl stared blankly. "I don't know. I can't remember."

"Don't worry! Got it!" The voice came from somewhere near the foot of the bed. "There's a nametape on the cardigan she was wearing. Carol Legat. That right, dear?" A second face appeared in front of her.

"Carol? Your name's Carol Legat, isn't it, dear?"

"I suppose so." If they'd said her name was Minnie Mouse or Marilyn Monroe it would have been all the same to her. She tried out the name: "Carol Legat." It didn't mean anything to her, but if that was what they said, then they were probably right. She would remember in a little while, but at the moment her mind refused to function.

"What am I doing here?" she asked. "What happened? Where am I?"

"Questions! Questions!" clucked the first nurse. "You're in St Christopher's Hospital and you've broken your leg. You were involved in a car accident. Can you remember anything about it?"

"No. I don't remember anything." Her mind was like a black velvet curtain, drawn against the past.

"It seems you were walking along a country road in the dark and a car hit you. Don't worry if you don't remember. It will all come back to you in time."

From the Recovery ward she was wheeled into a large general ward, then put by herself in a side ward off it. During the following day she had several visits from white-coated doctors, who examined her head, gazed with instruments into her eyes and ears, asked her questions and frowned at her replies.

"I don't remember. I don't know what I was doing on a country road in the dark. I can't even remember my own name."

The name Carol Legat on her cardigan meant nothing to her. She wondered if it could really be her name, but the hospital needed something for their records, so she accepted it for the time being.

"Any name would seem unfamiliar to you at present," one doctor told her. "Don't worry. Something will jog your memory soon and it'll come back; either in bits and pieces over a few days, or all together like a great blinding flash of realisation."

What concerned them more, he told Carol, was that no one had come forward to claim her. The accident had been reported to the police, of course, and there had been a news item on television, yet no one had reported a missing daughter, wife, sister or anyone remotely answering to her description.

"As soon as someone turns up who knows you, then you are sure to begin recalling things," he assured her. "In the meantime, have a look through your handbag. Perhaps there is something there that would trigger a memory." He picked up a black, leather shoulder-bag from the locker beside her, and laid it on the bed before departing to continue his rounds. The bag was well-worn but had been of good quality. With some hesitation Carol pulled it towards her and unzipped it, tipping the contents on to the bed beside her.

Inside was the expected collection of lipstick, comb, small mirror, packet of tissues and a pen, and in addition there was a key that was clearly a front door key, on a key-ring shaped like a shamrock, and a purse containing four pound coins and a small amount of change.

Carol picked up the mirror with mingled excitement and curiosity. It had occurred to her that she didn't even remember what she looked like!

About twenty-one or two, she looked, with dark, curly hair surrounding her head like a cap, rumpled and untidy now. Instinctively she reached for the comb and pulled it through the tangle.

5

Her eyes were blue, a deep, almost violet colour. She looked pale and there were shadows under her eyes and in the hollows beneath her cheekbones. But then, she had been ill, hadn't she? How ill and for how long she didn't know. They'd set her leg and that seemed to be the only obvious injury, but the doctors were still concerned about her. There was nothing to indicate any bang on her head and she felt quite normal, except that where there should have been the knowledge of who she was and where she had been going, there was only a blank.

Carol looked down at her hands. Ringless, so presumably she wasn't married or engaged. But wasn't there *anyone* in her life who would be worried about her by now? Surely, these days it was impossible to be missed without someone making enquiries? Did she have no relatives or friends at all? It seemed unlikely.

While she was trying to improve her appearance with the aid of the lipstick, there came a brief knock on the door and a man entered.

"Hallo! How are you feeling now?"

They always said that, Carol reflected. She looked up, noticing that this one wasn't wearing a white coat, like most of the medical staff. He was decidedly better looking, too, than any of the other doctors who had been to see her. A ripple of excitement ran through her as she took in his brown, wavy hair, sharp, intelligent-looking face with alert, brown eyes. He was tall, with the slim, muscular build of a man who led an active life; not an ounce of excess weight marred the line of his expensive-looking casual slacks and sweater.

"My leg still throbs a bit, but apart from that, and a few aches and bruises, I'm feeling fine," Carol smiled at him. "What kind of doctor are you? I've seen so many, but I don't think I've ever seen you before, have I?"

He sat down on the edge of the bed. "I'm not a doctor. My name's Luke Mackenzie. I was responsible for your being here and I came to see how you were progressing."

"That was kind of you. I'm afraid I don't remember much about what happened," Carol replied.

"I don't suppose you would. You were out cold. I thought you were dead at first. In fact, part of the reason I came was to reassure myself that you really were still alive."

"I'm alive. At least, I suppose I am." The remark sounded ridiculous, and she added quickly, "You see — I don't remember anything. Where I was, what I was doing — anything. Please tell me exactly what happened."

"I was driving along a country lane; near Oswestry, it was. Sometime between eleven and midnight, I should think. Suddenly, there you were, right in front of me and running straight towards my car. I suppose you must have been dazzled by the headlights. I slammed on my brakes and swerved but the offside wing caught you and threw you on to the road."

"You mean, you knocked me down with your car?" Carol asked.

"I'm very sorry, but I had no chance to avoid you. You seemed to be running straight at me. You couldn't have seen me at all."

"That's all right," Carol said mechanically, "I'm not too damaged and I'm sure you did all you could."

"I was horrified when I saw you lying there in the road. I thought I'd killed you. Luckily, I remembered seeing a 'phone box by the crossroads a little way back, so I called an ambulance and they came very quickly. Even so, it felt like the longest few minutes of my life."

"I'm all right now, really. Just a broken leg and a few bruises," Carol reassured him.

"Thank God for that! You were unconscious the whole time, of course, and I'd no means of knowing what damage had been done."

"There is one thing, though," Carol said. "I seem to have lost my memory.

Not only do I not remember anything about the accident, I've no idea what I was doing on that road at that time of night — where I was going, where I was coming from — anything."

"Really? How awful! But surely that will only be temporary? Won't your family and friends be able to remind you of things?"

"I don't appear to have any family or friends," Carol confessed. "The hospital hasn't been able to trace anyone who knows me. You see, I don't even know my own name."

"What! But I thought — " Luke appeared startled.

"There was a name on a cardigan I was wearing, so the hospital assumed that was my name," Carol explained. "But I don't know whether it is or not. It doesn't seem like my name."

"So you're not Carol Legat?"

"I suppose I must be. Only it sounds — funny. Not me at all."

"A rather ordinary name for such a pretty girl, I must agree," Luke said.

"It doesn't do you justice. You should have a romantic name, like Francesca, or Esmerelda, or something. That's the kind of name I'd give you."

Carol blushed and giggled. "No, I'm sure they must be right. My name must be Carol Legat. It's just that — nothing sounds like me. I don't even know what I'm like myself. I woke up fully to the world yesterday and I feel like a newborn person, with no memories, no past at all."

"Someone will be bound to turn up who knows you and can fill you in with all the details you don't know," Luke assured her.

"No one's turned up yet. Apparently no one's reported me missing or recognised me from the description they put out. It would seem they're all glad to be rid of me or I am a friendless orphan."

"I can't believe that! Perhaps your folks are away, taking a winter holiday and don't know you're missing. It's only just a week after New Year, after all;

still holiday for some. Someone will be along to claim you in a day or so."

Claim me like a piece of lost property, Carol thought forlornly. As the days passed and no one made any enquiries about her, she was forced to the chilling realisation that to all intents and purposes she had disappeared completely and no one seemed to care at all.

One person did show he cared, however. Luke dropped in most evenings to see how she was, and stayed chatting to her until the end of visiting hours. Carol told herself he must be feeling responsible for having run her down in the first place, but if it were only that, he didn't need to keep reassuring himself once he'd established that her leg was mending satisfactorily. The police had accepted that he had not been in any way negligent, and there was no question of his having been drinking that night. From what Luke had told her, and the report of the accident which the police had shown her, Carol was convinced she had been entirely to blame. She had appeared without warning in the middle of the road, right in front of Luke's car, and she had only his quick reactions and skilful driving to thank for the fact that she was not more seriously injured.

One evening, Luke brought with him a large photo album. "Let's see if any of these pictures stir a chord in your memory," he said. "These are all snaps I've taken of the area near my cottage. The road where you were walking is no more than seven or eight miles from it, so it's likely you came from nearby. There was no abandoned car found, and no one's come forward with any information about giving a lift to someone of your description, so we can take it you were on foot. You *must* have a local connection."

Carol took the album and slowly turned the pages. There were pictures of attractive countryside, some churches and old buildings, but none of them meant anything to her.

"No, I'm sorry," she said regretfully. "It was a nice idea, but I don't think I've ever been in this part of the country before."

"Shrewsbury," Luke said. "If you lived anywhere near here you must have been to Shrewsbury at some time. It's a very memorable town. There are several pictures of the old buildings at the end of the album. See if one of them reminds you of anything."

"It looks very nice," Carol said, turning the pages. "But I feel quite sure I've never seen any of them before. But what's that?" She stopped at a photograph of a pretty, chocolate-box cottage, with climbing roses and tiny, casement windows.

"Don't tell me that's the place you recognise!" Luke exclaimed. "That's my own cottage, and it's very well hidden, tucked away up a narrow private lane. If you'd ever seen it before, I'm sure I ought to know you."

"No, I'm sure I haven't seen it before," Carol said. "But the picture caught my eye because it was so pretty. Do you really live in a lovely little cottage like that?"

"It is nice, isn't it? And it's very comfortable and modern inside, too. I bought it originally for weekends but lately I find I've been staying there on a permanent basis. It's not all that far from this hospital, actually. When you're feeling up to it, perhaps they'll let me take you out there for a drive. A car trip would be much more likely to jog your memory than these snapshots."

"That sounds like a marvellous idea," Carol enthused. "It's terribly good of you to take so much trouble. I'd have been very lonely here if it hadn't been for you, visiting me so often."

"Getting your memory back has become a kind of challenge," Luke said. "And I feel responsible, in a way. After all, if I hadn't come along that road, you wouldn't have ended up in hospital with your leg in plaster."

"I might have ended up somewhere

far worse," Carol said soberly. "My leg's nearly better now but my memory shows no signs of coming back. The doctors are now saying that it's most likely my amnesia and the accident were not connected. They think there's a distinct possibility that I might have lost my memory some time before I walked into your car. The odd thing is, it seems there's nowhere I could have come from or have been going to. I might have been wandering about for some time; apparently my shoes were very wet and muddy, and they think I could have been miles from anywhere *because* I lost my memory."

"That's even more of a challenge," Luke said. "Where did you come from? What made you lose your memory? Why hasn't someone claimed you? I can't wait to solve the mystery."

"You've been very kind," Carol said. "But I can't involve you any more. You weren't responsible for my memory. Besides, I expect I'll be leaving here before long."

"What will happen to you then?" Luke asked.

"I don't know. But I don't need any more nursing and they said they need the bed. Probably my memory will come back any day now that the rest of me is healing, and then I'll know where to go."

Luke looked at her thoughtfully, but said nothing.

One afternoon, a few days later, Carol greeted him at the hospital entrance.

"Look! I can walk with just a stick!" she called. "And I don't suppose I'll need that for more than a short while. I have to practise walking around all the time, to strengthen my leg. They said I'm to be discharged next week."

"Discharged? But where will you go?" Luke stopped and looked at her in some concern.

"The hospital social workers have been ever so helpful. They've found me a live-in job as a housekeeper," Carol told him. "It seems I'm rather good at domestic work. I've been helping out

17

in the ward, doing the washing-up and bringing round the tea-trolley to the other patients. It gives me something to do and I enjoy it."

"Do you really want to take this job as a housekeeper?" Luke asked. "Living with strangers? Suppose you don't get on with these people?"

"I've really no choice," Carol replied. "I'm very lucky to have been offered somewhere with accommodation. You see, I don't know what skills I have, so I can hardly expect to find a job that pays enough to keep me, unless I live in."

Luke took her arm and guided her to a bench seat in an alcove off the hospital entrance hall.

"Look, Carol," he said hesitantly. "If you're prepared to be some stranger's housekeeper, why not come and be mine?"

"Yours?" Carol stared at him blankly.

"I genuinely need someone to look after the cottage for me. You saw the photo of it and you were clearly very taken with the look of it. I'd pay you whatever the other people are offering and at least you could feel you weren't going to a complete stranger."

"You don't need to do this," Carol said, taken aback. "You've been more than kind already. You've visited here so often, and tried to help me remember — "

"I'm not being kind," Luke broke in. "As I said, I do, genuinely, need a housekeeper. Although I've been spending more time at the cottage of late, I often have to go up to London and stay for a few days. And, this time of the year particularly, it's not a good idea to leave the place empty."

"But, Luke — " Carol began.

"I know what you're going to say. I can assure you that I'm not acting out of any feeling of responsibility towards you. I don't blame myself for your accident and I hope I'm right in believing that you don't blame me either?"

"Of course I don't blame you!" Carol exclaimed. "It was entirely my fault and

I have you to thank that I wasn't more badly hurt. Any other driver on that road and I might very well have been killed."

"You don't need to feel grateful, either," Luke said. "I have to confess that my visits here haven't been entirely altruistic. You're a very attractive young woman, and good company. Added to which, I'm intrigued by your story. I want to find out who you are and what you were doing, almost as much as you do."

"Well then, if you really need a housekeeper, I accept," Carol said. "I don't know very much about you, but then I don't know anything at all about this other family."

"You won't find it hard work," Luke said. "The cottage has been completely modernised inside. I've plenty of domestic gadgets as I'm not over fond of domestic chores myself. I'm not a fussy eater and I prefer plain cooking. When I'm not at home you can do as you please. Treat the place as your own."

"It sounds an ideal arrangement." Cautiously, Carol asked, "Is — is it only yourself I'll be keeping house for, then?"

"Yes. Just myself." Luke looked at her keenly and added. "There's no catch in this. I really do need someone — I'd have to advertise sooner or later anyway, and I'd rather have you than take my chance with a complete stranger from an agency. And, from your point of view, my knowing your circumstances and being sympathetic to them would surely be preferable to going somewhere where your loss of memory would be an embarrassment."

"That's true. I hadn't thought what a freak I could appear to people. No one would easily believe I've forgotten everything about myself."

"That's settled, then. And I promise I'll try to help you remember," Luke said. "Anything I can think of that might jog your memory. Perhaps we could take a few trips out when I'm free, and see if we can do some sleuthing."

"Thank you, Luke."

"I admit a mystery always appeals to me," Luke continued. "I'd like to know who you really are; but for the present *who* you are now, Carol Legat, is enough for me."

It was the end of the following week that Luke came to collect Carol on her discharge from hospital.

"Have you got everything?" He picked up the walking-stick and held it out to her. She shook her head.

"I shan't need that any more. I've been walking round the hospital grounds without it for two days. I'm completely recovered now."

"Well, where's your case?"

She laughed ruefully and held out a plastic carrier bag. "This is all, and quite light enough for me to manage. The hospital gave me a toothbrush and spare nightdress. Otherwise, I've nothing but what I stand up in."

Luke was visibly shocked. "That was tactless of me! It hadn't sunk in that you'd have nothing here. We'll have to get you kitted out properly. First stop must be some shops. I'll take you in to Shrewsbury and we can lunch there before going on to the cottage."

It felt strange to be driving along the roads again after her weeks in hospital. There had been snow in the last few days and Carol gazed at the sparkling hedges with wonder.

"It all looks so beautiful — I feel I'm seeing the world for the first time!" she whispered.

"Surely you haven't forgotten things like fields and hedges — and snow?" Luke laughed. "But I agree, the countryside does look attractive when the first fall comes. I must say I have a townsman's attitude to the country. I like it in summer but I prefer to stay warmly inside in bad weather."

Their first stop was at a large department store in Shrewsbury.

"Buy whatever you need. I'll tell them to charge it to my account. Don't forget you're buying for a whole new life; you'll need several outfits," Luke told her.

"Thank you. You can deduct it out of my wages over the next few months," Carol replied, conscious that she had only the four pound coins in her handbag, apparently the only money she possessed.

"Nonsense! I can afford a few clothes for my staff! Go ahead and indulge yourself in some pretty things."

Carol looked down at the clothes she was wearing. They were what she had had on when she had been taken to hospital; a plain navy coat, some mid-heel black shoes and underneath, a grey skirt, white blouse and a navy cardigan. She was very aware that she looked drab and dowdy. I must have had no dress sense at all, she thought. Which is very odd, because I do know what sort of clothes would suit me.

She chose a pretty, blue dress as an indulgence, then a couple of practical but smart skirts with toning blouses, a pair of slacks and a sweater, some shoes and several sets of underwear. Luke had wandered off, having sorted out the payment arrangements with the assistant. She sought him out and brought him back to the counter, eagerly showing him her purchases.

"I'm afraid this is going to come to an awful lot of money. I don't think I could ever have bought so many clothes, all at once."

"Doesn't look all that many to me!" Luke ran a critical eye over the nearest display racks and pulled out another dress and some jeans. "I should think you'd look good in these. Don't worry about the cost! I can well afford it and,remember, there aren't any clothes shops nearby when you're at the cottage. Tell you what: if you turn out to be a rich heiress you can pay me back, otherwise consider it as part of your wages." He nodded approval when she showed him the blue dress. "That will suit you very well. Put it on now instead of that thing you're wearing."

They came out of the store laden with packages. "Lunch now. There's a nice pub I know of, which does a good meal," Luke said. "We'll dump this lot in the back of the car and eat in comfort."

After an excellent lunch at an attractive old inn where Luke seemed to be well known to the staff, they drove on to the cottage.

Luke left the main road after some ten miles and took to narrow, winding lanes banked with high hedges. Carol had no idea where they were, and had ceased even to look out for any signposts. At last, he turned up an even narrower track which ended in a gate, before which was a turning space of rough ground.

"Here we are!" he announced. "Not quite like the picture in my album, I'm afraid, in this weather."

"But it's beautiful! Oh, Luke!" Carol breathed, clambering out of the car and hurrying to the gate. Before her was the cottage, its slate roof covered with a powdering of snow, the windows diamond-paned casements like the windows of a doll's house. The garden was a sheet of pure white snow, not a footprint sullying the path to the porch.

"Glad you still like it!" Luke was collecting the pile of carrier-bags they'd accumulated. "Here's the key. Let yourself in, please. My hands are full."

Carol fairly danced up the winding path to the green front door, half-hidden in the depths of the porch. As she slipped the key into the lock she saw there were ledges on either side, within the porch, and the thought came to her that here they might sit, on warm summer evenings, and enjoy the garden ablaze with colour as it had been in the picture in Luke's album. She knew at once she was going to love living in the little cottage.

"The layout's quite simple — you're in the living-room and the kitchen's beyond. Stairs on the right lead up to two bedrooms and the bathroom. That's all there is, apart from a lean-to beyond the kitchen. The front bedroom's mine. I'm sorry I can't give you a choice of view, but in summer the back garden is as colourful jungle as the front." Luke dropped the parcels by the foot of the stairs and went across to the fireplace. There was a wood-burning stove already alight, which accounted, Carol realised, for the unexpectedly cosy warmth which welcomed her.

"Good fire, this. It warms the whole house and you'll find there's plenty of hot water when you need it." Luke had opened the doors of the stove and stood warming himself. Carol walked through into the kitchen and stood, amazed, at the array of modern appliances which met her gaze. A washing machine, microwave and the latest of split-level cookers gleamed from all sides. Either Luke's previous domestic help had been a marvel at cleaning, or all this equipment was brand-new and barely used.

"Have you been here long?" she asked, automatically starting to fill the kettle.

"About two years. It was virtually derelict when I bought it. The kitchen's been entirely rebuilt and enlarged, and all the plumbing and rewiring is new." Luke came through to join her. "By the time the workmen had finished and I'd got it as I wanted, it might have been cheaper to build from scratch, but then I'd never have managed to keep the old look to the outside. I gather you approve?"

"I'm overwhelmed," she confessed. "I hope you're going to tell me how all these things work, before you turn me loose in here."

Luke laughed. "I see you're making tea already. A girl after my own heart! Come and see the rest of it while the kettle boils."

He carried the parcels upstairs and led the way into the back bedroom. It was a charming room, simply furnished with the bare essentials of wardrobe, chest of drawers and single bed, but the curtains and bed-cover were patterned with bright sprays of spring flowers and a large, furry rug covered the polished floor.

"What a lovely room!" Carol exclaimed.

"Glad you like it. This is my room, across the passage." He opened a door and Carol glimpsed a double bed and some rather lovely walnut furniture. Under the window, a huge desk, covered with papers and typewriter, dominated the room.

"I work in here usually. It's more convenient to shut myself away than have all my files down in the living-room," Luke explained.

"That kettle will have boiled. I'll make some tea. And when do you usually eat in the evening?" Carol asked, determined to establish her position as housekeeper. She did not want to appear to take advantage of Luke's easy-going attitude. With the slightest encouragement, he might easily forget he was employing her to run his

30

home, and would be treating her like a house-guest.

"About half past seven suit you?" Luke suggested.

"If that's when *you'd* like it," she answered primly. "I saw the freezer was full and you've got a huge larder, so I shall enjoy making you something special, as a thank-you for — for everything. The lucky thing about my loss of memory," she continued, "is that I don't seem to have forgotten how to prepare a meal. I think I must have been quite domesticated and the knowledge has become second nature."

In the kitchen, while she found cups, teapot and milk-jug, she pondered her natural aptitude for working in a home. It could point to her being a housewife, a married woman with a husband and perhaps even a child, somewhere. She looked down at her left hand. There was no mark where a wedding-ring might have been, but these days that did not necessarily signify. She shook her head. Somehow, she couldn't see herself married to anyone. A husband, even an unsatisfactory one, would surely have made enquiries by now, about a missing wife. There would be photographs, wedding photographs, published in the papers. She knew the police and the hospital staff had kept a close watch on reports of all missing persons: there could be no one from her past, seeking her.

Remembering is like trying to see through a brick wall, she told herself. Perhaps my memory will begin to come back in a while, now that I'm better from the injuries. And if not — She wouldn't think about that. The past might turn out to be something she would sooner not remember; the doctors had warned her of that. And as for now, the present was enough and the future looked as if it might make up for everything.

2

CAROL awakened early the next day, the sun on the snow throwing up a dazzling light which filled her room. She lay in bed for a few moments, collecting her thoughts, savouring the comfort and prettiness of her surroundings.

A glance at the bedside clock showed her that it was nearly seven. She could hear no sounds from Luke's room across the passage, so, careful not to wake him, she took her turn in the bathroom.

She was halfway through preparing bacon, eggs and coffee when he appeared at the kitchen door.

"To be awakened by such a scent!" he exclaimed. "Sheer decadent heaven for someone used to doing his own cooking. I overslept. I meant to clear away some work that's been accumulating on my desk over the last few weeks."

"You can do that after breakfast. Now that you've engaged me as your housekeeper you've no other commitments." Carol laid two places at the kitchen table and put a plate of bacon and eggs at one of them.

"I wonder if I ever worked in a motorway cafe," she added casually. "I seem to have fried those eggs rather well, and without even thinking about it."

Luke gave her a searching look before taking his place. "It still worries you a lot, doesn't it?" he asked.

"There's nothing I can do about it. Perhaps one day it'll come back — who knows? Perhaps I'm better off not knowing." Carol sat opposite him and began buttering a piece of toast. "Perhaps I'm a wanted criminal — a mass murderess. Had you thought of that?"

"Frankly, no. But then, so might I be, come to that. You never thought to enquire about me, did you?" Luke grinned at her across the table and

Carol smiled back. "You don't look like one, and I suppose one could say, 'it takes one to know one', so we're both unlikely candidates," she replied.

"I must say you are remarkably cheerful this morning. Doesn't your leg give you any more problems now?"

"Only a slight twinge occasionally," Carol admitted. "But this place has a good effect on me. I felt happy as soon as I saw the cottage. There are good vibes here. Can you understand what I mean?"

"Yes. I know exactly what you mean. I felt it too, as soon as I saw this place. That's why I bought it. I had to have it, even though it was an over-priced ruin when I first saw it." Luke stood up, his breakfast finished. "Look, I'll be working upstairs for a few hours, then I have to go out. I probably won't be back until about six. Do be careful if you go out; it looks slippery and your leg must still be a bit weak, in spite of what you say. You don't want to go breaking the other one."

"I'll be careful," Carol promised.

After Luke had gone, she washed up the breakfast things and pottered round the cottage, dusting and tidying. Later, when he had left the house, she chose a detective novel from the bookcase in the living-room and read until it was time to think about preparing an evening meal. She had fun experimenting with the cooker and microwave. To her delight, she found a large and varied stock of foodstuff in the freezer and was able to welcome Luke's return with a deliciously savoury casserole, followed by a rum trifle.

"I see I picked a good cook," Luke said appreciatively, as she brought coffee into the living-room afterwards. "I shall be driven to taking up jogging soon, or my waistline will double its girth."

Carol smiled her thanks, noting the trim, muscular body under his casual slacks and sweater. It would take more than a few good meals before Luke became flabby or paunchy.

"You don't seem to have deprived

36

yourself before," she said. "The place is full of stores. You'd have cooked them for yourself, I imagine, if I wasn't here."

"Probably." He wasn't listening, stirring his coffee with a thoughtful expression in his eyes. "Carol," he said at last. "I've been thinking. In a week or so I'll have dealt with the bulk of my work and be well ahead. And by then the weather may have improved. I'll take a couple of days off and we'll explore all the area round here, within a radius of — say, twenty miles or so. We're bound to come across somewhere you knew before you walked into my car. Even if it doesn't jog your memory, there must be someone who knows you, who will recognise you . . . "

"Thanks. But I doubt if it'll be any use. No one came forward when my picture was flashed on the TV screen. There can't be anyone to claim me."

"I'm not thinking of family or relatives. Someone in a shop, perhaps, might remember you as a customer.

That would give us a clue as to which area to concentrate on. And seeing someone is very different from recognising them from a quick look at a picture on the television. You'll see, we'll be bound to solve the mystery if we persevere."

"I don't know why you're taking so much trouble over me," Carol said, her voice quivering a little. "You're even more keen to find out who I am, than I am!"

"I can't resist a mystery," Luke said. "The world is full of them; great mysteries like the *Marie Celeste*, the Bermuda Triangle, or what became of the Romanovs. They're tantalising because they'll probably never be solved. But I'm sure the mystery of Carol Legat will be."

"I'm not at all sure that I want it to be," Carol said thoughtfully. "I'm happy here, and I'm getting used to the name Carol Legat. What if the answer was something I'd rather not know?"

"You can't not want to know!" Luke

exclaimed. "My dear girl — part of the reason I offered you the job as my housekeeper was the mystery about you, waiting to be unravelled! I must admit, the idea wouldn't have seemed quite so appealing if you'd been middle-aged and not so damnably attractive."

"Thanks for your honesty," Carol said drily. "I should have guessed, I suppose, that solving mysteries was a big thing with you. You've a shelf full of detective stories. Brand-new ones, by the look of them."

"Oh, you've been looking at my books, have you? And reading them?" Luke's hand dropped on to the novel she had left lying on the sofa.

"They say one can judge a person's character by the books he reads," Carol said lightly. "And all that shelf is by the same author. You *must* be keen on who-dunits!"

"You didn't look at them too closely, it would seem." Luke picked up the book and turned it over. On the back of the dust-jacket was a studio portrait of the author. Carol stared at it and then back at him.

"You!" she said. "You mean — you wrote all those books? *You* are Gerald Williams?"

Luke nodded. "That's the pen-name I use. Did you not know I was a writer? I thought I'd mentioned it."

"I assumed you were a businessman of some sort," Carol stammered. Her memory might be faulty over her personal details, but she knew well enough that Gerald Williams was a household name in the world of bestsellers.

"Writing *is* a business," Luke said with a shrug. "If you like reading my type of novel, feel free to help yourself to any on the shelf. But no comments, please. I can't stand discussing my work with anyone."

Later, they watched some television. There was a brief announcement that 'the mystery girl found wandering on a lonely country lane, has now left hospital'. Carol was relieved that no

40

mention was made of where she was now living. She was beginning to realise that she was in no hurry to be claimed by anyone.

"I'm going to do a few hours work before bedtime," Luke announced, after the news had finished. "I'll see you for breakfast about half past eight."

The room seemed a little lonely after he'd left. Carol picked up the thriller again but couldn't settle to it. She sat, staring at his picture on the dust-jacket, a studio portrait taken some years before. A strong face, good-looking and confident, the sort of man readers would associate with the hero of the novel.

She was suddenly afraid of what might happen if her true identity came to light. Here, she was Carol Legat, someone like a heroine in a novel, living in this lovely cottage with a handsome hero — and if anyone ever turned up and identified her, or remembered who she really was, there would be another life to return to, and this one would end. She couldn't believe that her past could be anything like as pleasant as Carol Legat's future promised to be.

Slowly, she got up at last and made her way upstairs to the pretty, flowery bedroom. Light gleamed under Luke's door and she heard the sound of his typewriter keys tapping long into the night.

One morning, some days later, Luke came into the kitchen with a satisfied smile on his face. He held up a fat, brown envelope.

"See, the manuscript's ready at last for my editor. All I need do is drop this into the post office and then I'm giving myself a holiday for a few days."

"You've finished your novel? That's wonderful!" Carol turned from the cooker, where she was frying bacon, to smile her delight.

"Considering the extra distractions of a young female about the place, I think I'm to be congratulated on getting so much work done in the time." Luke sat down at the table and began pouring himself some coffee.

"Well! I like that! I've saved you *hours* of time you'd have had to spend getting your own meals and cleaning this place!" Carol replied, with mock seriousness. She scooped the bacon on to a plate and slapped it down in front of him. "If that's all the gratitude I get, I hope this chokes you."

He caught her wrist before she could move away. "I *am* grateful, Carol," he said quietly.

She flushed. "I was only joking," she muttered.

"And to show you how grateful I am for all the good cooking and the sparkling clean cottage, let me tell you what I plan to do." He tried a mouthful of bacon. "Mmm, delicious! Now that the snow's mostly gone and the weather seems settled for a while, I plan to take you on some tours of the district and see if we can't jog that memory of yours into some sort of action."

The jokeyness went out of her, to

be replaced by a strong feeling of disquiet.

"Thank you, Luke," she said dully. "It would be nice to get to know the countryside around here, but please don't pin your hopes on my recognising anywhere, and getting my memory back. I think if I was going to remember, I would have had some glimmerings by now."

"We can but see," Luke shrugged. "Even if nowhere means anything to you, at least that could indicate that you're not from round here at all. Perhaps you were brought in a car — "

"Perhaps anything!" Carol broke in crossly. "Please, Luke, I don't want to speculate. If my memory is to come back, it'll come back of itself. It's not going to be jogged by any theories about what might, or might not, have happened."

"I'm sorry. I should have realised," Luke said, his face showing his concern. "It must be absolute hell for you, living in a vacuum like this, not knowing who might be worried about you. Come on, pack a few sandwiches and a flask of coffee and we'll get going as soon as possible."

In spite of her doubts, Carol soon began to enjoy the trip. At first, Luke drove through some attractive small villages, past isolated farms in the middle of bare fields, speckled with the melting snow to an attractive tweed-like colour.

"It's a lovely part of the country," Carol remarked. "I wish I did come from somewhere like this, but the places are all new to me. There's nowhere that looks at all familiar."

"Look at the churches, or the village shops, or the old war memorials," Luke suggested. "Anything that's distinctive; that might strike you as familiar."

"I have been looking. I've looked at everything we've passed," Carol replied. "I haven't seen the outside world for weeks. I was unconscious when I arrived in hospital and, apart from your bringing me to the cottage, I've seen nothing since then, until now. This is a splendid day out even if it doesn't produce any memories."

Luke came to a junction and turned off the main road. After some miles he slowed the car and pulled over on to the verge.

"Coffee?" Carol offered, since he was sitting there without saying anything.

"That might be nice." He accepted the mug from her and sipped it in silence.

"Anything to eat? You don't want to start our sandwiches yet, do you?" Carol asked at length. Luke seemed disinclined to drive on, yet there seemed nothing special about this piece of road. It was merely a narrow, winding lane without even a proper space for parking, so really he should not have stopped.

"Well?" Luke broke the silence.

"Well what?" she countered. "It's just a road between fields, with a little wood in the distance. Hardly worth stopping for the view."

"So it doesn't mean anything special for you?"

She looked at him, comprehension dawning. "You mean — *this* is where you found me?"

Luke nodded. "This is about twenty yards from where I actually knocked you down. You were walking along the road towards me, no, running, I would say, right down the middle of the road, and then, as my lights picked you out, you seemed to come straight at me, to run straight into the car."

"Was I dazzled by the lights, do you suppose?" Carol had a strange, detached feeling, as if they were talking about someone else.

"Let's retrace your steps. Coming?" Luke got out of the car and, somewhat unwillingly, Carol followed him. He led the way along the edge of the grass verge, then stopped and looked down at the road.

"Those marks could be my skid," he said, pointing. "Though its too long ago now to be sure. I expect the snow has washed away any other signs."

Carol shuddered. There might have been blood-stains that night, her blood, on the car and on the road. There was no evidence of that now, of course, on either place. Even the bruises and grazings she had sustained that night had all healed now and left no traces.

"This place doesn't mean a thing to me," she said. "It's just a strip of country lane in the middle of anywhere. It looks just like any other bit of road."

"I'm going to drive on slowly; back along the route you must have come. Have a close look as we go. There might just be something." Luke started back towards the car.

"But it was dark!" Carol protested. "You said it was nearly midnight. I wouldn't have seen anything."

"Was there a moon?" Luke stopped and turned back to her.

"How should I know? I told you, I don't even remember being here," Carol snapped. "Let's move on. It's pointless coming back here." But Luke was eagerly thumbing through a small, black book. "It was the end of the year — I haven't got last year's diary but I expect I could work it out from this month. Ah! I remember now! It had been raining heavily earlier. Probably clouds obscuring whatever moon there was." He tucked away the diary in his breast pocket. "It's hardly reasonable to expect you to recognise anywhere now. It would all look so different by night, anyway." He settled himself in the car again and started the engine.

The car rolled slowly back on to the road and Carol glanced idly out of the passenger window, without much interest. This place meant nothing to her and she couldn't share Luke's enthusiasm for investigation. Just before the car picked up speed again, they passed a gap in the hedge, filled by a stile and a footpath leading down through the field to a small wood away to the left. Suddenly, there *was* something. Leaning forward, she looked towards the wood and had a feeling, not a memory, it was not nearly as definite as that, but a feeling, a sensation of fear, almost blind panic.

"Luke," she said. "Let's stop this and get right away from this place. It's hopeless. And it's getting cold, too."

"You're right." Luke pressed the accelerator and the car gathered speed. "We'll stop for something to eat at the first convenient pub. Why, Carol, you look quite frozen, my poor child."

She must be looking rather white, Carol conceded, judging by the odd sensation that the wood had evoked. The feeling was too vague, too insubstantial to explain to Luke, and yet it was there. There was something frightening connected with that innocent-looking patch of trees.

They stopped at a pretty country pub and had some lunch. The day, though crisply cold, was sunny with a hint of the spring that was to come.

"This has been a lovely day out, Luke," Carol told him shyly. "I don't know when I've enjoyed myself so much. I — " She was suddenly struck by the incongruity of the remark. "How silly of me!" she said with a forced laugh. "Of course, I don't remember any other outings. But what I meant was — "

Luke put his hand over hers and pressed it. "It's all right. I know what you mean. We all come out with these meaningless clichés at times. I've only to look at your face to know you're happy and that's enough thanks for me."

There was a path from the back of the pub, leading down to the river, and after they'd lunched they wandered beside the water, looking out over reedbeds to the fields beyond, with peaceful cows standing at the water's edge. After a short while, Luke took her hand and kept hold of it until they finally returned to the car.

"Where now?" he asked, starting the engine. "I'm beginning to realise the countryside looks too similar to stir memories easily. Let's try a town. Shrewsbury, or one of the smaller places?"

"What if it does seem familiar?" Carol countered. "Where does that get us? It doesn't mean that I have friends or relatives there. It might look familiar merely because I'd seen pictures of it in a book, or on TV. I wouldn't know the difference, would I?"

"Point taken. I'm sorry if I appear obsessed with trying to trace your past," Luke said. "You're quite right that I shouldn't try to force things. I'm being stupid about it. I should have realised, if I trace your family I stand to lose a delightful companion as well as a splendid housekeeper."

"Dr Wilson said I might have lost my memory because there were things I didn't want to remember," Carol said. "He was sure that it was not caused by the accident, though that might have delayed its return. He thought I might have had a shock of some sort before the accident. I could have been running away from something."

"Or somebody," Luke added, very quietly. "Carol, my dear, it's beginning to look to me as if I might be doing you a great disservice in trying to reawake your memory. Let's give it a rest. If anyone eventually turns up who recognises you — that will be the time to try to remember. Until then — count your blessings. You've no regrets, no sorrows or unhappy reminders to spoil your present. That must be worth a great deal."

"And you — you don't mind having a mystery woman in your employ?" Carol asked.

"You're not such a mystery woman as you think," Luke said. "I've learnt a lot about you these last few weeks. I know what you're like, and I like what I've discovered."

"Thank you, Luke. It means a lot to me to be accepted as I am now," Carol replied.

"So! Where shall we go? Why not a trip to the sea? How do you fancy Rhyl without the tourists?"

It was still cold, with a sharp wind coming off the sea, but they ran along the empty beach like a couple of children, throwing pebbles into the waves, scratching messages on the wet sand, scuffling piles of it into rudimentary castles with flooded moats. The colour came back into Carol's cheeks and the fresh, salt-laden air was a tonic, sharpening her mind, her appetite and her enthusiasm for life.

They found, surprisingly, a cafe open and selling ice-cream, and had a giggly stroll through the town, licking cornets.

"Just imagine — the famous author away from his typewriter," Carol laughed. She paused outside a bookshop. "What would you do if they had a display of your books with your photograph in the window? You hardly look the part with ice-cream trickling down your chin!"

Luke produced a handkerchief and wiped his face. "I doubt anyone would recognise me from the photo on my dust-jackets. You barely did."

It was dark by the time they started for home. "Where shall we stop off for dinner?" Luke asked.

"No, don't let's stop. Let's go back to the cottage and I'll make us a special meal. I have an idea for a dish I'd like to try," Carol replied.

While she busied herself in the kitchen, Luke built up the log fire in the living-room and put a bottle of champagne to cool in an ice-bucket.

"I hope my cooking lives up to that," Carol said as she brought in a cloth and cutlery and proceeded to lay a small table.

"Bring it over near the fire." Luke moved the table so that they could eat sitting cosily on the sofa.

"This looks delicious! Wherever did you learn to cook like that?"

His stricken face turned towards her. "That was a terribly tactless clanger. I'm sorry. I didn't think."

Carol smiled back. "It doesn't matter. I *do* remember where I found this recipe. It was in an old magazine I was reading in the hospital. There was so little to do, and I had so much time on my hands, I read every word, including the cookery articles. It sounded so nice after the plain, institutional food we were served, that I suppose I remembered it so well."

They lingered over the champagne after the meal was finished. Luke leant back and put an arm round her shoulders, drawing her gently towards him.

"Carol, you'd stay here, wouldn't you, even if — " he hesitated. "You see, I'm beginning to look on you as a fixture here."

"I know I'd want to stay, whatever," Carol replied. "Even without remembering, I know I never could have been so contented, or felt so secure, as I do here in this cottage with you. I loved this place on sight. You remember how I seized on the photo of it when you brought me your album in hospital?"

His head was close to her shoulder,

resting against her.

"You're a comfortable person to be with," he murmured against her hair. "I'm so glad you're happy here. I'm so glad I found you." His lips touched her cheek, moving gently down towards her mouth. She turned towards him and his arms came round her. "Carol! Carol!" he whispered. Then his lips found hers and his kiss became more demanding.

A sudden frisson of fear ran through her entire body. She struggled away from him, pushing against his chest a with her free hand.

"NO! No, Luke!" There was blind panic in her eyes.

He backed away, startled. "What's wrong? Carol — my dear — "

"Don't! Don't!" she pushed frantically at him, pummelling his chest with her fists.

Luke stood up and moved out of range. "I'm sorry," he said stiffly. "I didn't realise it would offend you so much. It was sincerely meant, you know. I wasn't planning to seduce you.

I hope you realise that."

"Oh, Luke!" The tears flooded down her face. "I'm sorry. I'm sorry, Luke. I didn't know why I did that. I didn't mean it. Oh, Luke, I didn't mean to upset you." She was mortified by her behaviour. Why on earth had she reacted in that way? She *liked* Luke. Ever since he had held her hand by the river, that afternoon, she had wondered . . . she had been half hoping he might kiss her. Now *this*!

"I think we could do with some coffee. I'll make it," Luke said abruptly. He went out to the kitchen and shut the door between them.

Mopping up her tears, Carol tried to sort out what had happened. Everything had been fine until Luke had tried to kiss her. Just before his lips touched hers, when his face had been close, she had suddenly felt this unaccountable terror.

Her mind told her there was absolutely no reason for it. She trusted Luke; it had never occurred to her to be in the slightest degree nervous about living alone with him in the cottage. Though he treated her more as a companion than a housekeeper, she had always felt completely safe when she was with him. He was, after all, her only anchor in the world at present, the one person who cared enough for her well-being to take time and trouble to help her discover her true identity. She regretted bitterly how she must have hurt his feelings, but her reaction had been instinctive, and, she was sure, had had nothing whatever to do with him personally.

Luke came back into the room with two cups of coffee on a tray. He put one cup on a small table beside her and took the other over to the armchair by the fireplace.

"Thank you," Carol whispered meekly, sipping the hot, strong liquid. Luke had not spoken and she looked at him nervously.

"Luke — " she began.

"It's all right, Carol. You needn't apologise any more." There was a cold

59

formality about his words which she hadn't heard before.

"But I want to explain! It wasn't you — it wasn't you *at all*. I don't know why I behaved like that. I didn't mean to. I didn't want to — "

"Drop it, Carol. I said it's all right. I understand."

"Do you?" she asked wretchedly.

Luke finished his coffee and stood up. "You've had a long day and you aren't used to doing so much. You're overtired. Have a lie-in tomorrow. If I'm hungry, I'll get myself some breakfast and you can come down when you feel ready. Goodnight."

Kind words, but they only served to make her feel worse. He didn't understand, but they why should he when she didn't understand herself what had prompted her behaviour? It had something to do with her past, that much seemed plausible. And Dr Wilson had said her loss of memory might have been caused by some experience she preferred to forget.

When, eventually, Carol went upstairs to her room, there was no light under Luke's door, and the silent typewriter felt like a reproach, so used was she to hearing it in the night.

She sat on her bed for a long time, still thinking about the episode. If she was going to have any more inexplicable reactions to a perfectly natural affectionate gesture like Luke's kiss, she had better get herself sorted out before she made things so difficult for them both that she'd have to leave the cottage.

Wearily, she picked up the handbag that was her only link with the past. She tipped the contents on to the bed. Lipstick, comb, handkerchief, coin purse. All commonplace, all meaningless.

She plunged her hand into the now empty bag, pulling out the lining. The stitching had come apart at one corner, making a tiny hole. As she lifted the bag, she thought she heard a faint rattle.

She felt around the bottom of

the bag, between the lining and the leather. Something hard rolled under her fingertips. Gently she eased it towards the hole and worked it through. Then she was staring at it, lying in the palm of her hand.

It was a ring, a valuable one too, even Carol recognised that; a beautiful diamond cluster, the large central stone surrounded by perfectly matched smaller diamonds.

Instinctively, she slipped it on her finger. As she expected, it was a perfect fit. She stretched out her hand, twisting it this way and that, admiring the way the stones flashed fire in the light from the bedside lamp.

And then it hit her. A ring like this was, without any doubt at all, an engagement ring. She had even slipped it, without thinking, on to the third finger of her left hand.

And it was hers. She was quite sure of that. She sat staring at it as the shocked realisation of its implications flooded over her.

3

SHE was awakened next morning by Luke, gently shaking her. "Carol — I've brought you some tea. Wake up, sleepy-head, it's nearly nine o'clock."

Carol sat up quickly, concerned that she'd overslept, but a wave of dizziness and a throbbing head forced her to lie back again.

"You must have been tired," Luke said, putting the cup down on the beside table. He peered at her more closely. "I say, are you all right? You look a bit groggy."

"I feel awful," Carol admitted. "I'm sorry, Luke. I've overslept dreadfully. Give me a moment and I'll be down to cook your breakfast." The very thought of cooking bacon made her feel queasy.

"Don't worry about that. I've already had something. You must have drunk more of that champagne yesterday than I realised."

"I can't be used to alcohol," she said faintly.

"Well, don't worry about getting up yet. Drink your tea and come down when you're ready. There's no hurry."

When he'd gone, she took a tentative sip of tea. After half a cupful, nausea swept over her and she had to make a hurried dash for the bathroom.

Afterwards, when she'd washed and dressed, she felt very much better and went downstairs to find Luke in the kitchen coping very efficiently with the coffee percolator.

"Um, you look a lot better than you did earlier," he commented. "Want it black this morning?"

"Please. And I think some dry toast." Luke was clearly intending to ignore last night's incident, and she decided the best thing was to follow his lead and say no more. Carol picked up the loaf to cut herself some bread but he forestalled her.

"I'll make your toast. You sit down. No need to rush around this morning."

Carol sipped her coffee cautiously and nibbled a corner of toast. "Are you still on holiday?" she asked. "I thought you'd be back at work today."

"The answer's yes and no to that question." Luke poured himself another cup of coffee and explained, "I've had a letter from my publisher this morning. He wants to see me in London, so I plan to go up by train and stop over for the night. I'd suggest you came with me, but I don't suppose you feel up to it. Thing is, do you think you'll be all right here by yourself?"

"Of course I will!" Carol said promptly. "Isn't that what you're supposed to be employing me for, to look after the cottage while you're away? I only had a teeny bit of a hangover. I'm all right now."

"I'll drive to the station and leave the car in the car park, unless you'd like me to leave it here for you to use while I'm away?" Luke said.

"I'm not sure whether I'm entitled to drive. There was no driver's licence in my handbag," Carol replied. Mention of her handbag reminded her of the ring she'd found last night. She ought to tell Luke, yet she didn't want to. It was so clearly an engagement ring, but she couldn't accept that there must be someone, somewhere, whom she had been planning to marry; someone she loved presumably, and who loved her. She felt sure she ought to know if there had ever been someone special in her life. She had lain awake for a long time last night, thinking about that ring. She had pondered quite a few things, like how had it come to be under the lining of her bag, instead of on her finger? And if there was a fiancé who had given her a valuable engagement ring, why hadn't he come forward by now?

" . . . So I'll be back tomorrow night, providing everything goes to plan," Luke was saying. "Carol, are you sure you're all right? Have you heard a word I've been saying?"

"Yes — yes. Of course I'm all right. I was thinking — it'll be useful, you being away. I'll spend the time sorting out the larder and the deep-freeze."

"If that's your idea of a fun time!" Luke teased her gently. "I'd better be off if I'm to catch the train. Look after yourself." Luke went upstairs to collect his briefcase and overnight bag, and Carol began automatically collecting up the coffee cups.

It was quiet in the cottage after Luke had gone. Carol missed the sound of the typewriter though she enjoyed herself pottering about in the kitchen. At lunchtime, she tried bread and cheese but the queasiness came back and she settled for sipping some of Luke's soda water instead.

I didn't have all that much to drink last night, she reflected. Perhaps I ate something that disagreed with me, though if so, it's odd that Luke hasn't been affected, too. Maybe I'm coming down with a bug of some sort.

Later in the afternoon she went for

a walk in the woods at the back of the cottage. It was a pleasant, sunny day, though there was a cold wind. By the time dusk was drawing in, she had built up the wood fire in the living-room, made herself a bowl of soup and was planning to watch some television.

She managed to finish the soup and became absorbed in the evening's TV programmes. It was rather nice in one way to have the cottage all to herself; she could stretch out full length on the sofa and please herself entirely which channel she watched or when she ate. By seven o'clock she was feeling hungry again, so she got up to draw the curtains and prepare some supper.

The day had turned to rain, which spattered against the windows. The wind blew round the cottage and made little wailing sounds, lashing the tops of the trees at the back of the house. She was suddenly not so enthusiastic about being by herself and very conscious that the cottage had no near neighbours and there was not even a telephone installed.

Carol went into the kitchen and switched on the light. She picked up the kettle and took it over to the sink to fill it. Glancing up at the window, she found herself staring straight at a face, grotesquely distorted, staring back at her from outside. In fright she dropped the kettle and backed away. The face did not move; contorted, inhuman, it pressed against the window.

The scream came soundlessly from her throat. She stood, rigid with fear. The face moved slightly and she realised that its grotesque appearance came from the fact that it was pressed against the glass, the nose flattened, the lips thick and the cheeks bloodless. A few inches away from the window the face became human, but none the less frightening.

It was a man, a stranger, and he looked cruel and sinister. He moved away to the right hand and she knew at once he was going to try the back door. She rushed across the kitchen, through the door into the little lean-to where wellingtons, heavy raincoats and, of late, the spade for clearing the snow, were stored. She stumbled over the latter and fell on her knees on to a pile of logs Luke had left conveniently for her to use while he was away. She flung herself against the outer door, just as she heard the handle rattle. She slid the bolt, and felt the door move as she did so. Fingers trembling, she turned the key for good measure. Only then did she call out: "Who's there?"

There was no reply, only a muffled laugh and the sound of shuffling feet moving on down the path. Carol scrambled back into the kitchen and shut the door. There was a bolt on it, dating from the time before the lean-to, when it had been the outside door, so she bolted that, too.

She pulled the curtains in front of the window at the sink. They were not intended for drawing and barely covered the window but anything was better than having that face staring in at her. She picked up the kettle before she remembered the front door. She had never even noticed whether it was locked or not. Carol ran into the hall and threw the bolts on that door, too, and heard as she did so, the shuffling footsteps entering the porch.

She had already drawn the living-room curtains, but she ran quickly to check that the windows were all secured. They were casement style and the latches were old and lose. Even though fastened, a determined intruder could probably force them easily enough.

She was not safe here, even with the doors and windows shut and bolted. Carol ran upstairs and tried to look out of Luke's window to see what the man was doing now, but he was hidden from view by the porch, as he tried the front door. Then she sheard him shuffle on to the living-room windows.

Strangely, he didn't try them, but pressed his face against the glass, trying to see into the room. The curtains there were thick and after a moment he moved on, round the side of the cottage.

Carefully, Carol closed Luke's window and crossed the passage to her own room. From here she could distinctly hear the back door being rattled again. Those bolts are dreadfully old, she thought, in fear. He could pull them off quite easily, or smash a window and undo the catch.

She waited for the man's next move. It seemed an age of silence, and then she heard him go back round the side of the house again. Moments later, she thought she heard the click of the gate latch at the end of the path. Carol hardly dared hope, but there were no further sounds and it seemed that he must finally have given up and gone away. Even so, she was still too afraid to go downstairs again, or undress and get into bed. Dragging a blanket round herself, she curled up in the bedroom chair, ears alert for any sound of the wound-be intruder returning.

The cottage grew cold as the night

wore on. Eventually, Carol dozed and, just before dawn, staggered sleepily across to her bed, falling asleep fully clothed on top of it.

She woke at full light, cold and stiff. In daylight, it wasn't so frightening, though she still came downstairs warily. In the kitchen the light filtered dimly through the curtains. She pulled them back and picked up the kettle from where she had dropped it last night. Coffee and some toast revived her, though she still felt uncomfortable from having slept in her clothes.

After breakfast she had a long bath, indulging herself in the luxury of bath oils. The cottage needed cleaning and there were groceries to be bought before Luke returned.

Immersed in housework, Carol managed to put thoughts of the previous night behind her. She felt foolish now at being frightened and decided against mentioning it to the gossipy, middle-aged woman who served behind the counter in the local village store.

Mrs Braithwaite not only knew everyone in the village, but all about them too. Luke was the local celebrity and she followed his career with interest.

"Mr Mackenzie still writing his books?" she asked Carol conversationally. "Can't say I care for thrillers myself, but my husband enjoys them."

"There'll be another one out soon, I'm sure. He's away in London seeing his publishers about it now," Carol replied, finding it difficult not to respond to Mrs Braithwaite's chatter.

"Away? And you alone in the cottage? Don't you mind being all by yourself?"

"Mind? Why should I mind?" Carol spoke a little too defensively.

"Bit lonely, that place, with no other house nearby. It's a funny old world, these days." There was tantalising innuendo in those apparently unconnected observations. Mrs Braithwaite began stacking Carol's purchases into her shopping basket but it was clear she had more to say. Carol looked round for some way to prolong the conversation.

"Have you any ice-cream?"

"In this weather?" Nevertheless, Mrs Braithwaite delved into her freezer cabinet. "Only a family brick, my dear. That'd be too big for you, wouldn't it?"

"I'll take it. And some crisps. Salt and vinegar flavour. I'll take six bags."

Mrs Braithwaite's eyebrows shot up into her hairline but she made no comment. Sales had increased since Mr Mackenzie had engaged a housekeeper and it was not for her to speculate that in her experience attractive young women who kept house for good-looking and wealthy gentlemen were sometimes more than mere housekeepers.

"Tomato sauce," Carol said suddenly. "I'll take a bottle. Luke never uses it, but it's useful to have."

Luke, indeed!

"When's Mr Mackenzie coming home?" Mrs Braithwaite enquired.

"I'm expecting him tonight. He said he was going to spend some time checking research for his next book, so if he's late he might take the overnight train instead."

Mrs Braithwaite tucked the last of Carol's purchases into the shopping-basket, frowning disapproval.

"Now just you look after yourself," she muttered. "Be careful."

"What do you mean?"

"It was on the radio — chap attacked a girl yesterday, not too far from here. Police haven't caught him yet. I thought, with you being on your own — "

"I'll keep the doors bolted. Thank you for telling me, Mrs Braithwaite. I'll be all right."

Carol picked up the shopping-basket and walked slowly up the village street. In view of Mrs Braithwaite's tale, perhaps she ought to tell the police about last night's prowler. Yet now, in daylight and the safety of the village street, it didn't seem nearly so frightening. I must learn to stand on my own feet, she thought. If I report that man, it will make Luke think he ought not to leave me alone, and he hasn't the time to spend playing watchdog to me. I've given him reason enough to think I'm neurotic, as it is.

She passed the village policeman's house without stopping. The shopping-basket was heavier than she had expected and her leg, strong up till now, started to feel as if it might buckle under her. By the time she had trailed back to the cottage, a little over a mile from the village, she was exhausted.

It was past lunchtime and she was hungry but hadn't the energy to fix herself anything. She sat at the kitchen table and began eating one of the packets of crisps. Idly, she fished in her handbag and brought out the diamond ring, twisting it between finger and thumb so that the stones flashed fire.

Did I ever love him, Carol wondered. The ring brought no romantic stirrings in her heart now. If I loved him, he would have to be very much like Luke. The thought came unbidden into her head, and, because she was alone and with nothing else to do, she indulged in her day-dream. The kind of man she would marry would have to be self-confident and successful, like Luke, but he would have to have Luke's thoughtfulness, kindness and zest for life as well. Could there every really be another man just like Luke, in the world?

She glanced down at the table and was astonished to see she had absent-mindedly eaten half the family block of ice-cream. Six small empty bags round the plate proclaimed the fact that she had eaten all the crisps as well.

Good heavens, what a mixture! And I didn't even notice! I must be going mad! She picked up the rest of the carton of ice-cream and tossed it into the freezer. As she began unloading the shopping-basket, her stomach heaved and she had to dash for the bathroom.

I'm just not safe to be left alone, she thought, washing her face afterwards. I ate sensibly when Luke was here. I wasn't sick before I left hospital.

She put the ring away safely in

her purse. She still hadn't told Luke about it. She ought to have done, she knew, but she didn't want to. However much she co-operated with him in trying to unravel her past, she wanted to keep this unknown fiancé out of her life. He had no part in her present existence here in the cottage with Luke.

The day wore on. Carol kept herself occupied around the cottage but she had little energy and still felt queasy. She wandered into the garden where the fresh air made her feel better, and made a start on clearing away dead plants and leaves ready for spring. Snowdrops were already out, and clumps of crocuses beginning to show their mauve and yellow flowers. When the afternoon light faded, she went inside and opened the living-room fire, curling herself up on the sofa with tea and toast and one of Luke's books. She had no idea what time to expect him home, so there seemed no point in making any preparations for dinner; tea and toast was all she could face for herself at present.

As darkness fell, she drew the curtains everywhere, including the kitchen, and carefully checked all the outer doors were locked and bolted, and the windows latched.

She dozed over a TV programme, then returned to Luke's book but couldn't concentrate on it. She found herself listening for sounds outside, tensing at every rustle or snap of a twig. She hadn't realised there could be so many night sounds in the countryside.

At ten o'clock she decided Luke was unlikely to be coming that night after all, so she might as well go to bed. After uncomfortable time the previous night, she felt tired enough to sleep in spite of growing nervousness as the evening drew on.

Carol was halfway up the stairs when she heard the footsteps again, going round to the back of the house. She froze, her heart pounding. The back door rattled as the handle was tried, the door pushed and shaken. She listened while the footsteps passed slowly round the side of the house, to the front door facing her at the bottom of the stairs. She watched, mesmerised, as the handle turned, rattling against the door. There was a pause, an ominous silence while she held her breath, praying for him to go away, condemning her foolishness in not reporting this man to the police when she'd been in the village. What had Mrs Braithwaite said? A man on the prowl, attacking women? The police would have taken her seriously, not ridiculed her nervousness. Tomorrow she would visit the local village bobby straight after breakfast. Only tomorrow might be too late.

She heard a new sound. A scratching, scraping in the keyhole. Dear God! He's going to pick the lock! Her heart pounded with terror.

The door-handle was turned again, and pushed. She remembered the bolts and thanked heaven there were two, though both somewhat old.

Now came a thunderous tattoo on the door-knocker. Plucking up all her courage, she shouted, "Go away! Go away or I'll set the dogs on you! The police are watching this house. Go away or they'll arrest you!" Her voice ended in a squeak and she clung to the banisters, trembling.

"Carol! Stop playing silly beggars! Let me in. I've had a long day and I'm tired."

She flew down the stairs and tore at the bolts, fumbling in her haste to fling open the door.

"Luke! Luke!" She hurled herself into his arms, clinging to him and dragging him inside.

"Wow, that's some welcome," Luke murmured, gently trying to detach himself. "Do I need to ask if you've missed me?"

She broke away to slam the door shut, fastening the bolt and locks. "Oh, Luke, you've no idea how glad I am to see you!" she sobbed.

"Hey, what's wrong? Something's

82

frightened you — what's happened?" He put his arm round her and led her into the living-room.

"Sit down, Carol. Tell me all about it. Why, you're shaking all over!"

"I thought you were the intruder!" Bit by bit she told him. It seemed far less frightening now, with Luke there, sitting protectively beside her on the sofa, but he didn't smile when she'd finished.

"Did you manage to get a look at the man?" he asked.

"Not properly. When he looked in through the kitchen window his face was all squashed against the glass and it looked distorted. But I think I'd know him again, if I saw him."

"You have told the police, I suppose?"

"No. When I went to the village this morning I thought everyone would think I was being silly. I didn't think then he might come back again. All that about dogs and the police was just make-up."

"I should have had a telephone

installed," Luke said. "This place is far too isolated to be without one. But when I bought it, I deliberately chose to cut my links with the outside world. It was intended to be a hide-away, a place where I could get on with my work with the minimum of interruptions. I should have realised there would be disadvantages, too."

"I know I ought to have told the police," Carol said. "Mrs Braithwaite said there was an attacker prowling the district. But I didn't want to appear neurotic. I've done some silly enough things without risking getting the reputation of being thought a nutcase."

"No one would ever think you were that. There really was someone, wasn't there? You didn't imagine it," Luke reassured her. "Well, leave it to me. I'll talk to Constable Williams and if I'm away again he'll come up and check on the cottage."

"You must be starving!" Carol remembered and jumped up. "I'll get you something quick to eat."

"I had dinner on the train. All I'd like is a drink and then I'll stagger off to bed. When I found the place locked, I thought you must have gone to bed and be sound asleep, or else your memory had returned and you'd rushed off to be reunited with your relatives."

"No such luck," Carol said lightly. "I haven't remembered anything yet." Guiltily, she thought of the ring, still in her handbag. Right now was not the time to tell Luke, but tell him she ought. Still her mind rejected the idea. If he knew about the ring, its implications would change things between them. She looked across at him, sprawled in the other armchair, a glass in one hand, eyes drooping in utter weariness. In a few short weeks, this man had come to be very important to her. She hoped that, in time, perhaps she might become important to him. But if he thought there was another man in her life, one with a greater claim on her, he would never let her know his own feelings.

"Luke," she roused him as she took the glass from his fingers before it slipped to the floor. "There's a pile of mail came for you while you were away. Do you want to sort through it now?"

"Not particularly." He took the miscellaneous assortment of envelopes from her, riffling through them without interest. "Doesn't look as though there's much that's important. Bills and junk mail mostly. They can wait till tomorrow." He made to toss them on to the table, then checked himself. "No, wait a minute — there's one for you here."

"For me? How could there be?" Carol's heart began to pound. "Nobody knows I'm here." With fingers that trembled, she took the envelope Luke was holding out to her, and tore it open. She sighed with relief when she aw the official headed notepaper of the hospital.

"It's only an appointment for a final check-up to see that my leg's fully recovered," she said.

"I thought the local GP would do that sort of thing. When is the appointment, anyway?"

"Next week."

"That's a bit awkward for me. If it was early in the morning, perhaps I might manage — "

"No, it's all right. No need for you to be involved. I can easily get there by bus on my own. Really, Luke," Carol added as he began to protest. "It's about time you stopped treating me as if I were a child — or your guest. Anyway, I'd *prefer* to go by myself."

"Very well, if that's how you want it. I suppose it's only a routine check-up, isn't it? You're quite all right again now, aren't you?"

"Yes it is, and I am." She didn't show him the letter. They wanted to see her about her memory, too, of course, but she didn't want to discuss that. Let Luke think it was only her leg; he knew that was fully recovered. The truth was, she didn't want him to go there with her. Not if there were going to be investigations into her memory; he was far too keen on helping her try to remember the things she would far rather keep forgotten!

Luke scooped up his letters, and stood up. "I'm off to bed before I fall asleep down here. Breakfast about eight? I've a lot of work to catch up on."

On his way to the door he had to pass her chair. Casually, he pressed her shoulder, then dropped a light kiss on her cheek. "'Night, Carol. Thanks for looking after the place so well — and everything."

He was halfway upstairs before she could respond.

4

CAROL presented her appointment card at the desk of the out-patients' clinic. The place was busy; it looked as if she might have a long wait. She collected a magazine from a pile on a side table and sat down on a chair in a row outside a door marked with Dr Wilson's name. After some minutes a nurse came up to her.

"You have another appointment today, haven't you?" she asked. "You're seeing Dr Wilson now, about your accident injuries, then Dr Pearson this afternoon."

"I don't ever remember seeing a Dr Pearson when I was a patient here," Carol frowned. "Who is he, exactly?"

"Dr Pearson is head of our psychiatric department. Dr Wilson was sure your memory loss had nothing to do with the injuries you received in the car crash, so he asked Dr Pearson to see you. He is the best person to help you overcome whatever it is that is preventing you from remembering."

"But Dr Wilson said my memory would come back naturally, as I became stronger," Carol protested. "I'm very fit now."

"But it hasn't come back, has it? And problems of the mind aren't Dr Wilson's field. I'm sure you'll find Dr Pearson can help you," the nurse said encouragingly. "He knows a great deal about these things and he's a very nice, kind and sympathetic man."

Carol listened meekly while the nurse gave her directions where to find the psychiatric unit. There wasn't any point in arguing with her about keeping the appointment; she was being helpful and it really wasn't her concern, but, as she buried her head in the magazine she didn't want to read, Carol debated whether she should keep the appointment or not. Did she really want this man's help? At the back of her mind, on the very edge of memory, was still that sensation of fear. If they made her remember, she would bring on herself thoughts that her subconscious had been pushing out of her mind, protecting her from memories she didn't feel able to handle yet.

"Carol Legat!"

Her name called at last, she walked into Dr Wilson's office without having come to any decision.

"Hallo, Carol! It's nice to see you looking well. Sit down and tell me how things have been with you lately." Dr Wilson was a jovial, fatherly man who mended broken bones and patched up accident victims with great cheerfulness and kindness. She doubted if he would understand why she should be reluctant to know about her past.

Dr Wilson examined her leg, his skilful hands testing for weakness in the muscles and joints.

"That seems to be an excellent mend, Carol. You've done well. Any other problems?"

"Not with my leg. But I have had quite a lot of backache recently. And I've felt grotty — sick and listless. But I don't think that has anything to do with my leg," Carol replied.

"Backache, eh? Let me give you a thorough examination. Sometimes damage is slow to show up, though in this case it seems unlikely — nearly three months since the accident, wasn't it?"

She was back on the examining couch, Dr Wilson prodding and pressing, his practised hands examining her back and pelvis.

"It all seems to be in good order," he said at length. "But I'd like to do a few more tests. The nurse will take you to have a scan, and some blood samples. There's nothing to worry about," he added reassuringly. "We're studying new techniques all the time, and if you would help us by allowing us to take these extra tests, you'll be helping enormously in improving treatment for patients in the future. Go with the nurse now, she'll explain exactly what we want." Dr Wilson murmured something to the nurse which Carol did not catch, and then she was shepherded into another room. Blood and urine samples were taken speedily and efficiently, and then she was given a body scan.

"What are these new techniques?" she asked the nurse conversationally. "Surely, Dr Wilson would have done all this while I was in the hospital, when I first had the injuries?"

"Perhaps he did," the nurse shrugged. "They probably took lots of samples and did tests when you were having your leg set, whilst you were under the anaesthetic. They're always having new theories and trying new treatments. They don't tell us what they want samples for, but you can rest assured it's nothing bad for you. Dr Wilson told you you've recovered completely from all your injuries and you look very fit."

Her second appointment, with Dr Pearson, was not until the afternoon.

Carol found a cafe nearby and had some lunch, then strolled round the shops. It was nice to be out by herself in a place that boasted more than just Mrs Baithwaite's village stores.

She still hadn't come to any definite decision about seeing Dr Pearson, but somehow, she found herself drifting back to the hospital, following the nurse's directions to the psychiatric unit. Perhaps Dr Pearson could help her, if she could bring herself to talk to him, but if she didn't want to remember, surely he couldn't make her.

There were fewer people in the waiting-room and she was shown almost at once into the doctor's office. Dr Pearson greeted her in a friendly manner and indicated a comfortable chair for her, in front of his desk. He glanced through a folder of notes before him, then pushed them aside and turned his attention to Carol.

"How much do you remember? I mean, how far back can you go?" he asked.

"I remember waking up in hospital with my leg in plaster, and aching all over, with lots of bruises. I was told about Luke — Mr Mackenzie's — car hitting me, and much later, when I left hospital, we visited the place, though in daylight and I didn't recognise it at all. So you see, I have a mental picture of what happened, but that was because of what I was told, not because I remember it happening."

Dr Pearson nodded. "Tell me, you had a handbag with you when you were brought into hospital. At the time, the contents meant nothing to you, you said. But since then — has anything struck a chord?"

"Nothing in the bag was any help. They were just — things. Ordinary things, lipstick, comb. That sort of thing. And the clothes I had on — they were more like a uniform than real clothes. I thought — " she hesitated.

"Yes? Go on." Dr Pearson was not looking directly at her.

"I thought — if I was the kind of

person who wore those kind of clothes, it wasn't me. I mean — they weren't the sort of things the person I know I am now, would have worn. Oh, dear, that's very confusing. You must think I have some crazy ideas," Carol said.

"Not at all. That's very interesting. You may have thought, perhaps, that the clothes weren't yours?"

"Yes, something like that. Except that they *were* mine. I was wearing them and I hadn't any others so they had to be mine."

Dr Pearson made a brief note on a pad in front of him.

"Don't feel hesitant about saying just exactly what you feel, expressing your thoughts and impressions, however fanciful they may sound to you. Your mind gives out some seemingly nonsensical signals, as in dreams, but they ae all clues which have meaning when we study them." He paused, then added. "It's rather strange, don't you think, that the police were not able to trace anyone who knew you? Surely you must have friends and relations who would report your absence?"

"That's something I've wondered about, too."

Dr Pearson reached for the folder but as he did so there came a discreet tap on the door.

"Come in," he sighed.

A young woman in a white overall entered and handed him a folder. "We were told you were to have this at once. We'll have the results of the tests tomorrow, but as you can see, the pictures are very conclusive."

Dr Pearson laid the folder on his desk and opened it. He glanced up at Carol. "Please excuse me a moment. It seems something urgent has cropped up that needs my attention."

Carol nodded, glancing away to look round the room. Some other patient's notes, she guessed, more urgent than herself.

Dr Pearson nodded to the girl. "Thank you, Phyllis. Tell Dr Wilson I'll handle this, and thank him for passing on the information."

The girl left the room and Dr Pearson continued to study the folder for some minutes. At last, he pushed it aside as if he would deal with it later, and looked across at Carol.

"How have you been feeling lately?" he asked, as if their conversation had never been interrupted.

"Oh, very well. I told Dr Wilson that my leg felt fine now. He doesn't seem to have found any problems with it now. He said I'd make a complete recovery."

"Completely fit?" Dr Pearson looked at her from under bushy eyebrows. "Nothing at all you've noticed, not even unconnected with the accident injuries?"

Under his scrutiny Carol hesitated. "Well, I do occasionally have a slight backache, but that's just natural tiredness. Nothing to do with my leg."

"Anything else? Such as nausea, or bloated feeling? Weight gain?"

"I *have* put on weight, a bit. But

that's cooking for Luke, the gentleman I keep house for. He appreciates good food and I like cooking. I did feel a bit queasy occasionally shortly after I left hospital, but I don't at all now. In fact, I feel very well indeed."

"Carol," Dr Pearson clasped his hands on the desk in front of him and for the first time, looked at her directly. "I've been looking at the report from Dr Wilson. You had some further tests today, I believe?"

"Yes. Dr Wilson said it was something to do with new techniques to help other patients. It wasn't, was it?" There was a sense of foreboding, she could feel that Dr Pearson was holding something back from her. "I *am* all right, aren't I?" she asked, suddenly afraid. "You aren't going to tell me that I was hurt worse than they thought? I'm not permanently damaged, internally, am I?"

"Don't look so scared, Carol. There's nothing the matter with you. You're very fit. You said yourself you felt very well. What may come as something of a surprise to you, if you don't remember anything — we've discovered you're about three months pregnant."

"*What!*" She stared at him in total disbelief. "That can't be right! How could I be? It's impossible!"

"It surprised us, too, when we saw the foetus on the scan. That's why Dr Wilson had some extra tests done, urine samples taken. The results won't be ready for a day or so, but there's really no doubt about it. The scan was very conclusive."

"But how could I have become pregnant? I couldn't have, without knowing anything about it. I mean — I've never — " she floundered.

"But you cannot remember, you said. So you wouldn't have known, would you?"

"You mean — *how* long have I been pregnant?" Her brain was whirling. She couldn't take in what he was telling her.

"From the information we have, the foetus appears to be about three months.

That would date it to about the time you were admitted to hospital. Now, Carol, I know this has come as something of a shock, but, thinking back over the last couple of months, do you not think there might have been some suspicions in your mind? Little clues like the nausea, backache, and so on, which might have made you wonder?"

"It never crossed my mind for a second that I might be pregnant!" Carol declared. "And I still don't understand how I could be. If, as you say, I was pregnant when I was brought into hospital from the accident, why didn't anybody realise it then? I was X-rayed at the time, I imagine?"

"Yes, but calculating backwards, you could only have become pregnant a matter of a few days before. Perhaps even less. There was nothing to indicate it and no reason for the casualty staff to check. When you were brought in I suspect it would have been far too soon to have shown up in any tests, in any case."

"But what am I going to do? I'm still too astounded to think," Carol said.

"My dear, there's no reason to be upset. In fact, the very opposite. Doesn't it indicate to you that somewhere there must be someone who loves you very much, who is frantically trying to find you? We must step up enquiries about you, get back to the police, have your picture screened on television. Really, we should not have dropped enquiries at all. By now, we'd have traced where you come from, found your husband — "

"No!" Carol cried out. "I don't want you to find anyone! I don't want to find out who I am! I only want Luke!" She burst into a fit of sobbing.

Dr Pearson let her continue for a few minutes, then passed her a box of tissues without comment. He waited while Carol blew her nose and took a grip on herself, then he said kindly, "Luke, I take it, is Luke Mackenzie, with whom you took a post as housekeeper, isn't he? My dear, I have to explain to you that whatever your relationship with him is now, you only met Mr Mackenzie while you were here in hospital. He couldn't possibly be the father."

"Of course I know he's not the father!" Carol said indignantly. "Luke and I aren't lovers. I wish we were, but we're not. He's the only stable, real part of my existence. I *know* him. I don't know who in the past was responsible for this pregnancy, and I don't want to know. Whoever it is, I don't want him. I want Luke."

"How can you make any choices or decisions without knowing what the alternatives are?" Dr Pearson said. "Don't you see, now its imperative that you discover who and what lies in your past.Then, and only then, will you be able to decide what you want to do."

"I'm afraid," Carol said bluntly. "If I had had a happy relationship I'm sure I'd *know*. I'd feel — well, I'd just know. But I feel nothing; as though there had been no one until Luke came along."

"There are other things you haven't

considered," Dr Pearson went on. "This pregnancy isn't going to go away, like a touch of the 'flu. In a few months' time you'll have a baby to care for, another person who has needs and rights, too. Don't you think the baby might have a right to know its father, even if you insist on denying that father any right to knowing of this child's existence?"

"Oh, I don't know! I don't know *anything*!" Carol cried. "I need time to think about all this. I've barely taken in the fact that I'm having a baby at all."

"This Luke — you obviously have a close relationship. How do you think he will react to this news?" Dr Pearson asked the question with studied casualness.

"Luke! I couldn't tell him! I couldn't!" Carol was horrified at the idea.

"But you'll have to, eventually, if you intend continuing working as his housekeeper," said Dr Pearson. "You don't have much time; it will become obvious in a few weeks more. Then, whatever the future holds, he will surely want to help you trace the father, so that at least you'll be in a position to make decisions about the future for all of you. If you'd like me to help you — "

"I couldn't tell him. I just couldn't. I couldn't even tell him about the ring — " She stopped. Her eyes widened as she watched his face. Dr Pearson didn't always appear to pay much attention but he never missed anything that was said to him.

"Ring? What ring is this? I don't recall anything being said about a ring before. Carol, I think you haven't been entirely open with me about yourself. Shall we begin again and this time you tell me everything, everything you remember and everything you've discovered about yourself, even if you didn't remember about it? It's the only way. And we *must* find out the whole truth, now."

So she told him, about finding the ring, about her feelings of unhappiness and fear that seemed to be linked to it; about the vague uneasiness that enveloped her for no reason. Dr Pearson sat in silence, nodding occasionally, making a few notes on the pad but not speaking until she finally stopped.

"You think this ring is probably your engagement ring?" he asked. "Do you have it with you now?"

Reluctantly, she drew it out of her handbag. Dr Pearson held it between his fingers.

"Very pretty — and expensive," he commented. "Whoever gave you this would hardly have done so casually. He must care for you a great deal. Don't you want to wear it now?"

"No! I found it under the lining of the bag — doesn't that indicate that I was trying to hide it — that I didn't want to wear it then, either? I didn't just drop it into my bag, I stuffed it right to the bottom."

"It's a fairly distinctive design. I think we should try to arrange for this to be shown on the television news. Someone is very likely to recognise it. If not your husband, then a jeweller, or someone who knew you, saw you wearing it — there are several possibilities."

"No!" Carol snatched the ring back and thrust it into her bag. "Don't you understand? *I* don't want him found! I don't want to know who he is!"

"You have to be practical. Some time, near the end of September or so, you are going to become a mother, with a child depending on you for everything. In your present position, do you think you'll be able to keep the baby without some outside help?"

"I'll manage," she muttered.

"But for how long? One day your child will want to know about its father. What are you going to tell it?"

"I may have remembered by then. In which case, I shall know what to do."

"Carol, I think you remember more than you've led me to believe. I think you are trying to shut out memory when it would easily come back if you let it."

"I don't remember!" She screamed the words at him. "And I don't want to have memory forced on me! Leave me alone. I won't be pushed by you or anyone. I'll remember in my own time!" She jumped up. "I'm going now. And I don't want another appointment." More calmly, she added, "I know you've tried to be helpful, and I am grateful for all you've done for me. But I don't want anyone forced on me yet. I have enough to contend with, taking in what you've just told me."

"I understand. Well, I'm always here at the hospital if you need me," Dr Pearson said. "You can always reach me by telephone whenever you want. Just promise me one, no, two things, Carol."

"What are they?"

"Telephone the laboratory tomorrow for confirmation of your pregnancy. It looks conclusive but we ought to double check. And then, sign on for proper ante-natal care and make arrangements for the birth. It's only another six months and you'll need medical supervision. Don't just ignore it. It won't go away."

Carol nodded. "I'll be sensible. Just give me a little time." She backed towards the door. "I — I'm sorry I got a bit hysterical."

"That's all right. Carol — tell Luke. Tell him soon."

"I will when I'm ready. When I have to."

"He'll be a help to you, I'm sure of it. I met Mackenzie once and he impressed me very favourably. All this is too much for you to bear alone, if you won't let me help you."

"You won't trust me!" she burst out. "You'll force me to go on TV and have my pictures in the papers; you'll go on until this man appears and I'm not ready for him yet. I need a breathing space."

"Take one then. But remember, the baby won't wait for you. Keep in touch — and good luck."

Carol walked down the long, white,

highly polished corridors in a dream. It couldn't have happened. It couldn't be true! She went into the women's toilets near the entrance and in the privacy of the locked cubicle she pressed her hands over her abdomen. There was a hard, unyielding lump about the size of a fist, inside her. When she pressed it, it moved of its own accord. How, she wondered, could she not have noticed it before? It explained her previous aches, the nausea in the mornings, the cravings for odd food combinations, the tightness of her clothes. It really was true; she was pregnant and she hadn't the remotest idea who the father was.

In the pale sunshine of the early April afternoon, she sat in the well-tended hospital grounds and tried to plan how she would tell Luke. It wasn't as if she were confessing to infidelity, but it felt very much like it. And it was inevitably going to change everything; it must put Luke out of her reach for ever. And, even worse, if it did not, could she ever be sure that anything happened between them now, was not out of pity for her, rather than love?

It was late when Carol stepped off the bus in the village and and walked slowly up the road towards the lane to the cottage. She wished now that she had agreed to let Luke meet her with the car, as he had offered. She had been determined to be independent and not disrupt his work with the need for lifts. At least he had insisted on preparing the evening meal for both of them, in spite of her protestations that he was supposed to be employing her for that job. She still had not decided how she was to tell him her news, when she reached the top of the lane and saw the cottage in all its spring glory, in front of her.

Luke wasn't in the kitchen, but a deliciously savoury smell of food cooking greeted her. Carol went upstairs to take off her coat and change into more comfortable clothes. Knowledge made her conscious of her thickened waistline and to her eyes it now seemed very noticeable. She found a skirt with an elasticised waistband and pulled a baggy jumper over it.

There was no sound of the typewriter from Luke's room and she assumed he must have gone out. She went down to the living-room and was startled when he called to her from the depths of his usual armchair.

"Hallo, there! How did it go?"

"Oh — all right. My bones seem to have mended very satisfactorily." She braced herself, waiting for a suitable opening.

"Like a drink?" he asked. She saw he had a glass in his hand and there was a bottle on the hearth by his feet.

"Er — no, thanks. Supper smells delicious. I thought you'd be working upstairs."

"No. It wasn't going well. I spent the afternoon proving to you that I'm not totally helpless when it comes to cooking."

"I'm sorry. About the book not going well, I mean." Carol sat down on the sofa. If he was despondent about his work she couldn't burden him with her own news just yet.

"It'll sort itself out. Writers' block, it's called. Actually, it was an inability to concentrate on the thing."

"I hoped you'd get more work done if I was away. I've always thought you defeated the object of employing a housekeeper by spending too much time talking to me. And I'm sure you must have watched far more television since I came."

"I enjoy your company. It's good to have someone around when I take a break from my work. You're not an interruption — ever."

"Thanks. Luke, I — I wanted to tell you — "

He put down his glass and came across to sit beside her.

"You didn't only see the doctor about your leg, did you?"

"How did you know?" she asked. "I saw a psychiatrist, Dr Pearson. He told me — "

"I knew they'd be more concerned about your loss of memory than your broken bones. They usually leave the final signing off to a local GP, but I knew they'd want to check on your memory. Did they say whether they thought there'd been any improvement?"

"There's no change. My memory's the same as it was in hospital."

"Didn't they suggest anything you could do, that might help. Could they give you any idea how much longer you'll be like this? Do they realise what an impossible situation it is?"

"It may come back of its own accord, or it may not. That's all they can say. We'll just have to wait and see." Carol spoke lightly and was surprised by Luke's reaction.

"My poor darling! You must be going through hell, not knowing anything. I wish to God there was something I could do to help."

"I haven't been going through hell. I'm quite resigned to the way things are. I remember all I want to remember.

That's the part of my life since I came out of hospital. I don't care about anything else. I don't *want* to remember," Carol replied.

"How can you say that?"

"Because it's true. I — sense I was very unhappy then. Probably that's why I want to shut it out of my mind. I *know* I'm happier now than I ever was, because I feel as though I've come alive for the first time."

"Darling!" Luke's arms went round her and this time she did not flinch or move away. She let him hold her close, buying her face against his shoulder, longing to pour out her troubles, yet dreading to destroy the closeness they now had.

"Carol, my love, I've been sitting here all day, thinking about your appointment. That's the real reason I couldn't do any work."

"But why? Why should you be so worried about it?" Carol asked in surprise.

"Don't you see — I was *afraid* they'd

succeed in restoring your memory. It was selfish of me but I was so worried that, once you remembered, you'd go away, back to wherever it was, and I'd lose you. I've felt such a swine, hoping that you wouldn't remember, yet imagining what you must be going through, not remembering. Do you really mean to tell me that you don't mind about it?"

"I don't want to remember because if I don't, it doesn't exist," Carol said confusedly. "I remember everything since you first visited me in hospital. That's all I need. I have no other life."

"You've no idea how happy it makes me to hear you say that," Luke said. "Because you've become so important to me. I couldn't bear to lose you."

"You won't lose me. I'll never leave here unless you send me away."

"Why on earth should I ever want to do that?" He held her close again, kissing her lips, her throat, her eyelids, caressing her with a gentleness which strengthened into passion.

"Carol — I love you! I want you with me always," he murmured. "I've been so afraid that one day I was going to lose you."

Even as she snuggled against him, revelling in the glorious feeling of safety as his arms enfolded her, Carol's heart felt like lead. She couldn't tell him now; and yet she must. It couldn't wait much longer. Dr Pearson had warned her that very soon it would be noticeable and she must tell him before he realised it for himself.

"Luke, there's something I have to tell you." She struggled free and sat back against the cushions of the sofa, trying to marshal her thoughts.

"It can't be important, my love." He took her hand, pulling her towards him. "Come upstairs with me. Please, Carol. I want to love you. We can be married as soon as you like."

For a wild moment she was tempted. It would be so simple — let Luke make love to her, let him think the child was his — the reality was only too clear. She was three months pregnant; no way was he going to believe that the child could be his.

When he pulled her to her feet, she realised something else. If she let Luke make love to her now, he'd know she was pregnant. She had to tell him — and now.

"Luke, listen!"

Her anguished tones made him pause, and she managed to persuade him to sit down again, beside her.

"Please listen to me, Luke," she begged. "The doctors at the hospital ran some tests — and they — they found that I am pregnant!"

It was said now. She waited, holding her breath. Luke stared at her as if he did not understand what she had said.

"What?"

"They've taken some samples, but that was only to confirm what they saw on the scan. They were quite sure about it. I'm definitely pregnant."

"But that's impossible! They have made a mistake."

"I'm at least three months pregnant. I must have been pregnant when I ran into your car last January."

"You mean — all this time — ? Did you know about this? Did you suspect that you might be?"

"I had absolutely no idea. Such a thing never occurred to me for a moment. I was astonished when they told me."

"There must be some mistake," Luke said brusquely. "Tests can be wrong. They've confused you with another patient, or something. Didn't you tell them it was impossible?"

"No, Luke. The scan was quite clear. And, anyway, I'm sure they are right. It explains why I felt so grotty a while back, and why I've put on quite a bit of weight."

Luke nodded at her searchingly and with a sick misery she saw his expression change and harden.

"Doesn't this revelation bring back

anything to your memory? Surely, something as startling aṡ this is bound to stir your subconscious? Don't you know who the father is, Carol?"

"No, I don't." She was in tears now. "I don't remember how it happened, or who it happened with, or anything."

"My poor child." He rested a hand on her shoulder, but the touch and his tone were different now; caring still, but no longer full of passionate desire. he might have been an elder brother.

"You realise this makes all the difference? We *must* trace your people now. You need help, you need your family, and — and the father, whoever he is."

"But I don't! Can't you understand — I still don't want to go back, wherever 'back' is!" Carol shouted. "I *know* I wasn't happy then."

"You can't judge from these vague feelings you say you have. You're happy here, and this is the situation you know and understand, so it's natural you should want things to stay as they are, and to be fearful of something unknown. But you've no evidence that you weren't just as happy before. There's every reason to suppose a stable situation; happily married, with a good husband and starting a family." His eyes were bleak.

"I know I wasn't! And I know I wasn't married!" Carol thrust her left hand, fingers extended towards him. "Look! Not even the mark where a ring could have been!" she challenged.

"Even so, there's a man somewhere with whom you had a close and loving relationship. You aren't the type of girl who would ever indulge in casual sex, so I can't believe you felt nothing in return. There's another point. If not for the father's sake, at least you owe it to the baby to try to trace him, and to find out who you are. Could you bring a child into the world and tell it that not only will it not know who its father is, but it won't know who its mother is, either?"

"It's my decision," Carol began.

"Not any more. You're no longer on your own. You never were on your own, my love, but now you have the baby and that must come first. That's if you really are having a baby."

"There's no doubt about it. I'll telephone the hospital tomorrow for the results of the other tests they took, but there's no need. The scan was enough and — and I've felt it for myself. I — " she broke off to gasp, and clutched her stomach.

"I — I felt it move then," she whispered. "Oh, Luke, why did it have to happen? Who was it out there who caused all this? I only ever wanted you."

5

OVER the next few weeks Carol lived in the closely cocooned world familiar to expectant mothers. She developed a placid, unthinking attitude to the months ahead. As her body swelled and her waistline thickened, so her days passed uneventfully, in routine domesticity. Luke was kind and very caring towards her, but now he was the loving friend or brother. Gone was the eager light in his eyes, the glow of desire when he looked at her. Had she not been so totally absorbed by the changes taking place inside her, she would have been unable to bear living with him under these circumstances. She loved him; she yearned for him to love her as he had begun to do before he knew of the child, but her condition prevented her from feeling the sexual frustration she might otherwise have known. It was bad enough to see the desolation in his eyes when he looked at her, to listen to his deliberately impersonal conversation, the closeness gone between them. She was his housekeeper now, nothing more. The hospital had confirmed what she knew already and after that Luke had accepted the fact of her pregnancy and with it, reluctantly accepted that she was not prepared to co-operate in seeking out the father of her child. Carol simply did not want to know. It was as if the pregnancy had, for her, developed spontaneously; as far as she was concerned there wasn't and never had been, a man involved.

Luke's response was to spend more and more time at work in his room upstairs. It was, after all, for the purpose of giving him more time for work, that he had engaged a housekeeper in the first place. Except that he hadn't planned to have a housekeeper until he'd met Carol, and then the idea had become a little distorted.

"Carol, do you need a lift into the village this morning?" he asked, over breakfast one day.

"No thanks. I don't need to buy much. The walk to the shop will be good exercise." She collected the plates and began stacking them in the sink. Luke stood up. "I'll go up and start the day's work, then."

That conversation was typical of how they were now, Carol thought sadly. Polite, formal remarks as though they were hardly more than strangers. In an attempt to encourage something more, she asked, "How's the new novel going?"

"It's going quite well at the moment." He opened the door into the hall and Carol turned round from the sink, desperate to keep him a few more minutes. "Tell me about it. Tell me the story as far as you've got." If she could start him off telling her about this latest novel, perhaps some of that early closeness could be coaxed back.

"I'm sorry. I can't talk about my

books when I'm in the middle of them. I thought you realised that."

Luke shut the door behind him and Carol felt as if he were symbolically shutting her out from his life.

I'm being too sensitive, she thought. I take too much account of feelings which have no bearing on what's real. Dr Pearson was right; I ought to be more realistic. I should trace the father of this baby and sort everything out. I'd be free then, to come back — but would I? Would Luke still want me then?

She finished washing up the dishes, collected her purse, the shopping-bag and a cardigan and started off for the village shop.

Mrs Braithwaite eyed her with a mixture of disapproval and grudging respect. Carol was conscious that the bulge was not concealed by the loose blouse and cardigan she was wearing, but in this warm weather of early summer it would have drawn more attention to herself to have worn a coat.

"And how are we this morning?" Mrs Braithwaite greeted her. Carol was, after all, a good customer and Mr Mackenzie's housekeeper.

"I won't be buying any more ice-cream and cheese and onion crisps," Carol smiled. "The craving for peculiar food seems to have gone."

"Ay, folks is mostly fittest after the first three months." Mrs Braithwaite looked sideways at Carol and added, "And when is the bairn due, my dear?"

"Some time towards the end of September, the hospital thinks. Nobody's quite sure exactly when."

Mrs Braithwaite sniffed and proceeded to collect together the few items on Carol's shopping list. She was silent for an uncharacteristically long time, then, unable to resist her curiosity, said, "Going to be a wedding soon, is there? Quiet like, just you and him, maybe?"

"A wedding?" Carol looked mystified.

"Well, aren't you going to — ?" Mrs Braithwaite pursed her lips into a tight button of disapproval. "I know these days there's a lot of funny ideas about marriage, but what with Mr Mackenzie being well-known and that, I'd have thought he'd be somewhat the conventional sort."

The penny dropped and Carol flushed scarlet. "Oh, you've got it wrong, Mrs Braithwaite!" she burst out. "This baby isn't Luke's! I'm his housekeeper. Just that and nothing more, I assure you."

"Not Mr Mackenzie's?" The older woman's eyebrows shot up, to disappear under her hair. She paused in packing the shopping-bag and Carol realised she was not going to get out of the shop without some further explanation.

"I was pregnant before I came to work for Mr Mackenzie," she said. Then added rashly, hoping to discourage the woman's interest in scandal, "It seems I have a husband somewhere, but I lost my memory and can't remember anything about my past, and he hasn't come forward to claim me yet."

"Lost your memory!" Mrs Braithwaite's

manner changed from disapproval to sympathy. "You poor young lass! Whoever would abandon a nice young lady like you, and his own bairn, too! Wicked, I call it!"

"I'm sure there are good reasons, Mrs Braithwaite." Carol picked up her shopping-bag and stuffed the rest of her purchases into it. "Perhaps we've both lost our memories. I'm sure it will all be all right soon."

She hurried out of the shop, wondering what Mrs Braithwaite and the other village gossips would make of that for an explanation. Perhaps she had been unwise to say anything, but she could hardly have let Luke be blamed for her condition.

As she toiled back to the cottage, she reflected that this was the first time she had publicly admitted the possibility of having a husband. In spite of her pregnancy, and the engagement ring, she still refused to think of the necessity for there to have been a man involved.

When she reached the end of the lane leading to the cottage, she saw someone on the path near the front door. A man, a young man, was walking slowly past the windows. As he paused to cup his eyes and peer in, she was suddenly reminded of the prowler who had frightened her the first time she had been alone, and a wave of fear swept over her.

Carol backed slowly away from the fence that bordered the cottage front garden, still watching the man. She was sure it was the same man.

It was daytime now, and Luke should be in the cottage, but still she couldn't bring herself to go up the path and confront him. She watched him walk round to the back of the building and then she turned away. To her right was a path leading into a small wood. She ran along it, hiding herself among the young silver birches and sapling beech. From here she could see the roof of the cottage, but no more, and, finding a tree stump deep within the trees, she sat down to wait. She'd give him half an hour. Either he'd have gone by then, or Luke would have dealt with him, whoever he was. A tramp begging for food, she thought, or a gypsy, perhaps. He was scruffily dressed, though not ragged.

The minutes passed. Without a watch she was forced to estimate the time. When the tree stump finally became so uncomfortable that it was pleasanter to stand, she judged it might be safe to go back.

There was no sign of anyone when she emerged from the wood and looked cautiously towards the cottage. She went up the path and in at the back door, the entrance she normally used.

Everything seemed as usual, and there was the reassuring sound of Luke's typewriter coming from upstairs. She unpacked the shopping, then made a cup of coffee to take up to him.

"You've been a long time. Were you all right?" Luke glanced keenly at her as he took the cup. "You're looking a bit pale. It's too far for you to be walking all the way into the village now, especially with a shopping-bag."

"Luke — that prowler was round here again. Did you see him?"

"Prowler? Who do you mean?"

"The man who was wandering round the cottage the night you were in London. He was here again just now, peering through the windows again, like he did before. I was so scared I waited in the wood till he'd gone. Didn't you see him?" She spoke in a rush.

"Oh, *that* prowler! Don't worry about him. That was Jason," Luke said reassuringly.

"Jason? Who's Jason?"

"My brother."

"Your *brother*?" Carol stared in amazement. The peculiar creature who had terrified her was the last person on earth she would think of as Luke's brother.

"I should have explained to you about him," Luke said. "Sit down and I'll tell you. He's my kid brother, and he's always been a problem to the family. Right from before he was in his teens he was in and out of hot water at school. He was expelled from two of them. he got involved in drugs, thieving, violence, the lot, in his teens. Now he's twenty he's been in worse scrapes. He was in prison for six months and only came out at the end of the last year."

"How on earth could you have a brother like that?" Carol said. "So utterly different!"

"It's a long story. To be accurate, he's a half-brother. We share the same father, but different mothers. Jason mixed with bad company when he was young and he was an impressionable kid. That's about all you can say in his defence. He has no excuse for the mess he's got his life into. Now he's found out where I live, there's not much I can do to avoid him."

"What did he want?"

"Money, mainly. Since he came out of prison it seems he's been living rough. He's been doing odd jobs at the farms but at this time of year there's not been a lot of work. By chance, he discovered this was where I lived and I suppose he was having a look round when he frightened you. Not seeing me, he was put off, but today he finally found me and spun me a yarn about helping him go straight."

"Are you going to help him?"

"What else can I do? He's my brother, after all. I can't see him penniless when I have plenty. I'll have to do whatever I can for him," Luke shrugged.

"He's not coming to live here, is he?" Carol asked.

"Heavens, no! My family loyalties don't stretch to those extremes!" Luke gave her a reassuring hug. "Jason won't be encouraged to come round here again, especially if he frightens you so much. Whatever I do for him, part of the bargain will be for him to leave me in peace."

"He won't frighten me again. Not now I know who he is," Carol said. "I thought he was a monster at first.

I can laugh about it now, but he had his face squashed against the kitchen window-pane and it made him look barely human."

"Sometimes I think Jason *is* barely human," Luke muttered. "Certainly, he's not civilised. Look, Carol, I've told him I'll help him find work, away from his old cronies and his criminal past, on condition he doesn't contact them or resort to drugs and crime. Perhaps I'm expecting too much of him; I don't know. I'll have to risk that. But I'm afraid you'll have to bear with the fact that he may turn up here once more, to see me. We've arranged that I'll find him work and somewhere to live, reasonably near here so I can keep an eye on him, but not so near that he'll be an embarrassment. He'll probably come back in a week or so to find out if I've had any success. If I'm not here when he comes — "

"It's all right, Luke. I shan't be scared of him now. You've no need to worry about me on that account any more,"

Carol broke in. "If you're not here, I'll tell him he can wait for you. I'm sure I can handle that."

"Good girl! I wish you'd come in while he was still here; then you could have met him," Luke continued. "Jason's not such a monster when you know him. It's just his upbringing and background, and I suspect he was born without any sense of right and wrong. He's always taken what he wanted, without any consideration of the consequences."

"How come you're so different, yet you're closely related?" Carol asked curiously.

"My mother died soon after I was born. My father's work meant he had to travel extensively — he was agent for an international company — so he couldn't bring me up himself. I was brought up by an aunt. Not the proverbial old-fashioned maiden aunt, I'm glad to say. This one had five children of her own, so my cousins were more like brothers and sisters to me. We're all scattered over the world now, but we're still close and try to meet up whenever we can.

"Dad eventually married again; a rather different woman from my mother. Jason's mother, Sylvie, worked in a seedy night-club in South America and most of her family and all her friends came from the criminal underworld. I've never known why my father married her. Perhaps she became pregnant and he felt he should do the honourable thing; perhaps, even, Jason isn't really his son at all. I own I've sometimes wondered. Maybe dad was lonely and there's no denying Sylvie was a very attractive woman. My father died soon after Jason's birth and Sylvie and her dubious family brought him up. Otherwise, he might have turned out very differently. Dad left money in trust for both of us when we came of age — I was seventeen when he died — so Aunt Cath kept in touch with Jason. I suppose she felt a bit responsible for him, too, as her brother's other son.

Jason will inherit a sizeable amount soon, and by then I hope he's learnt a bit more sense, otherwise he'll get himself into even more trouble."

"I'm so sorry, Luke. I had no idea." Carol touched his arm gently. There had been a sadness in his eyes and she realised she was seeing a side of this self-confident, successful man that she had never suspected.

"He's not going to upset you, Carol. That I'm determined about. Jason has a vicious streak, I must confess. If he thought he'd frightened you from coming home while he was here, the idea would amuse him enormously. I've no doubt he was the prowler you spoke of, and I've no doubt that, realising I wasn't at home and that you were here alone, it gave him satisfaction to know he was frightening you. It's no comfort now, I know, but if you'd ignored him at the time, I'm sure he'd have given up and gone off much sooner."

"I'll remember in future. I won't be scared of him again."

In spite of her words, Carol shivered slightly at the memory of that lonely winter's night and the fear she had experienced then.

Luke put his arm round her. He hadn't shown such a gesture of affection for weeks, now. Not since she had come back from the hospital and told him about the baby.

"I'm here to protect you, my dear, and that's what I'll do, for as long as you need me," he told her.

"If only you would!" Suddenly, everything was too much to bear and she threw herself close against him, sobbing.

"Hey, Carol love, what's wrong?" He stroked her hair, calming her.

"Luke, I'm frightened *now*!" The words came muffled from against his chest.

"Little one, you've no need to be. There's a home for you here, for you and the baby, for as long as you want. As long as you need. You know I'd never let you down. You've become very dear to me, Carol. You know that, don't you?"

"Yes, Luke," she sniffed.

"Then there's no need to be afraid. I'll be with you. I'll even be with you when the baby comes, if you'd like that. But by then let's hope your memory will have returned, and then you'll have your real family to help you."

"I want to stay with you always. Please, Luke, say that I can always stay here, whatever happens," she said childishly, clinging to him, fearful of losing the one solid anchor in her life. Looking up at him, she was startled to see the desperate lines of unhappiness etched on his face.

"I've told you you can stay as long as you want, dear," he said. "But we can't go on like this for ever. We must resume efforts to find out who you are — "

"No!" In her anguish she struck at his chest with her fist. "Don't you understand? *I don't want to know!* I want to stay here with you! I love you,

140

Luke. I know I've never loved anyone, ever, like this. You don't have to marry me. Just let me stay here and cook and clean for you. Promise you'll never let me go. Promise, whatever happens, whoever claims me, you'll not let me go away from you. Promise!"

He stroked her hair, kissing her on her cheeks and throat, murmuring gentle, loving words to calm her. All the while as her frenzy subsided, she felt the tension in his body, an ache of misery which transferred itself to her.

"Carol, darling, you know there's nothing I'd like more than to know that you will be with me for always. I'd marry you tomorrow if I could. But you must realise that your very condition points to the fact that you can't be free. There simply *has* to be someone, some man who has a claim on you. You're not the sort of girl to have entered into a relationship casually, or been promiscuous. Don't you think I haven't thought about all this, been tortured by the thought of who the father of your baby is, and the fact that he *must* have a prior claim on you?"

"There's no one. I *know* there's no one I've made love to!" Carol declared.

"My dear girl! Do I have to give you a lecture on the facts of life? Whatever your feelings now, there *had* to have been someone, near the beginning of this year, with whom you made love. Accept it, Carol. I have. It was hard enough, and there's not a day goes by that I don't wish with all my heart that it could have been myself instead. But there's only one way out of this problem; find this man. I'm certain that he holds the key to unlock your memory. And then — "

"I don't *want* to remember!" Carol shouted. "I want things to stay as they are now. I want to be Carol Legat, your housekeeper, your lover, your whatever you will. But I don't want to be anyone else. I *won't* be anyone else!"

"And what about the baby? He — or she — has no name. No father's name and you're not even sure about his mother's name. You owe that at least to him, even if you won't try for yourself."

Luke handed her his handkerchief and while she blew noisily into it, he went on, "What are you afraid of? Do you think there could be anyone who would try to take the baby from you? That's not possible, under the law."

"Oh, you don't understand!" she threw at him in exasperation. "A name doesn't matter. If you think it does, why not give the baby yours — and me too, for that matter?"

"You know that's not possible." Luke stood up and his tone was cool. "You know we couldn't get a licence to marry without proof that you're not married already."

"Luke," Carol said in a quieter voice, "if — if I go back to Dr Pearson at the hospital and ask him to help me, would that be enough? Would you promise to leave the rest to sort itself out? I mean — do nothing else yourself to try to trace anyone?"

"You really would go back and co-operate with Dr Pearson? That's being sensible at last." He dropped a kiss on the top of her head. "It's a good start. Who knows, if he's successful, we may not need to do anything else. Now, go and make us some more coffee. We could do with it after that."

Carol went first to the bathroom to wash her face and clear away the marks of her emotional storm. She did not see Luke's face as he turned back to his typewriter. He looked like a man facing the torments of the rack.

The following day Carol walked down to the telephone kiosk in the village to keep her promise and make an appointment with Dr Pearson. She could not but feel relief when she was told there was a waiting-list for appointments and it might be several weeks before she could be fitted in.

"What did you say your name was?" the receptionist asked.

"Carol Legat. I was admitted to the hospital last January due to a road accident. But my memory loss wasn't connected with that at all — "

"I remember," the girl broke in. "I took the details when you had your last appointment, a few weeks back, wasn't it?" There was a pause and an indistinguishable murmur of voices at the other end of the line, and then the receptionist's voice came again, "I'm putting you through to Dr Pearson now."

There was a series of clicks and then the psychiatrist's voice. "Carol? Nice to hear from you. Has your memory come back?"

"Nothing's changed. But — I want you to help me remember." She had said it. There was no going back.

"Splendid! I'm sure that once we co-operate on this, things will begin to happen. Half the battle is wanting to remember."

"Luke says we can't go on indefinitely as things are. He wants me to sort out my past."

"I'm delighted to hear you've both

come to a sensible decision. And how are you feeling now? Much better? The baby coming along well, I trust?"

I wish he wasn't so hearty, Carol thought. "Can I make an appointment?" she asked.

"My secretary tells me my clinic appointments are fully booked for weeks ahead. But I'll tell you what I'll do, my dear. Your case interests me and it looks as if you need to consult me urgently. Can Mr Mackenzie bring you to my home one evening? I can see you privately."

"I don't know about that! I could hardly afford private fees! And Mr Mackenzie is my employer. I couldn't expect him to do that," Carol protested.

"Ask him! And, look. There'll be no consultation fees. As I said, your case interests me. It's very unusual for total amnesia to last this long without the slightest glimmer of memory returning, especially with a full return to health and a trauma-free lifestyle. I may write a paper on it. Anonymously, of course.

And I'd very much like the opportunity of meeting Mr Mackenzie. I've enjoyed his books enormously. Now, got a pencil handy? Here's my address ... "

Carol put down the receiver feeling she had been pressured into more than she had bargained for. An appointment weeks ahead was one thing, but a private session with Dr Pearson in four days' time was quite another!

When she told Luke about Dr Pearson's offer, he suggested driving her the twenty miles to the doctor's home, before she even had time to ask him.

"I'm relieved to know you are getting help at last," he said. "Of course, it's possible Pearson might suggest advertising in the national press. There must be people looking for you, too, and I imagine the reporters will seize on it as a good story, so you'll have to be prepared for some of them turning up here to ask for an interview."

"Interview? Why should they interview me?" Carol snapped irritably. "How can

I tell them anything? I've lost my memory. Remember?"

Luke gave her a long, hard look but said nothing. Carol had been moody ever since she had agreed to see Dr Pearson. He put it down to nerves but he could not rid his mind of a growing suspicion that had dogged his thoughts for the last few weeks. He welcomed the opportunity of talking to the psychiatrist himself about Carol's mental state; he had confidence that Dr Pearson would find out the truth of the matter.

The evening before the appointment, Luke suggested that they might go out to dinner afterwards, since they would be some distance from home.

"That's if you feel up to eating out," he added. "I don't know whether hypnosis, like a trance, will drain you of energy for a little while afterwards."

"Hypnosis?" Carol went rigid. "What do you mean, hypnosis?"

"That's what Dr Pearson will do. They should have tried it a long time ago, in the hospital before you were discharged, but I imagine they were more concerned then with getting your leg strong again — "

"I'm not being hypnotised," Carol said flatly.

Luke gave an amused laugh. "Dr Pearson is a psychiatrist. It won't be like those music-hall turns where someone takes away the chair that's supporting you, or anything daft like that. He'll merely talk to you, under hypnosis, and you'll remember, or your subconscious will remember — "

"I'm not going to let him hypnotise me," Carol insisted.

"Believe me, it's the only way. The facts are there, locked inside your mind — "

"Then they can stay locked. I don't want to know."

"I thought we'd been through all this," Luke sighed. "Carol, be sensible. You need to know. Whatever you felt for him, the father of your baby has a right to know about it. And you have a right to make claims on him."

"I don't. I wouldn't. I can bring the baby up myself."

"What if I insisted you traced him? I could force you. I could refuse to let you remain as my housekeeper when the baby arrives."

"I daresay there are other jobs!" Carol's hands trembled as she served their supper on to plates. They were in the kitchen, about to eat, and Luke realised, too late, that this was not the best time for a battle with Carol.

"You know, of course, that I wouldn't turn you out. Even if it was twins," he joked, in an attempt to lighten the atmosphere. "But we agreed, didn't we, that we had to make an effort to trace the man, or someone you knew."

"Not by hypnosis. I won't have him hypnotise me," Carol said. "If that's what he is going to do, you may as well cancel the appointment."

Luke's patience snapped. "I certainly won't! Dr Pearson has taken the trouble to make a special appointment for you.

150

He's put you ahead of others on the waiting-list and I am not going to be discourteous — or ungrateful — enough to turn down his offer."

"You go then," Carol retorted. "Because I won't. And if you try to make me, I'll refuse to co-operate. I've told you, I *won't* be hypnotised."

"Very well. I will keep the appointment by myself," Luke said. "I'll ask his advice — he might have some helpful suggestions as to how I can learn to deal with a difficult, wilful, stubborn child."

Luke kept his word, driving off next day alone. He left early, saying he would spend the morning in a large library, catching up with some research he needed for his book. The atmosphere between them had been cool since the previous evening, and Carol was almost relieved when the car disappeared down the lane and she was left alone.

She wondered what she should do with her day. She considered exploring the countryside nearby, but her increasing bulk made a long walk uncomfortable. She settled on a stroll through the wood with frequent rests whenever a convenient log or grassy bank presented itself.

Carol returned at midday and made herself some lunch. The day, which had been sunny earlier, became overcast and a spattering of rain put paid to the idea of sitting outside, so she settled herself with her feet up on the sofa in the living-room and opened one of Luke's thrillers.

She was totally absorbed in its exciting intrigues when she was abruptly brought back to reality by a loud rapping on the front door.

Few people ever used the front. She and Luke invariably went through the back door, where coats and wellingtons were stored, and their only callers were postmen or deliverymen, who, well-known to them both, often walked in, in the fashion of the country, to deposit their goods straight on to the kitchen table.

Carol went out into the hall and tried to see who was there. She pulled back the bolts and opened the door but there was no one standing in the porch. She stepped outside and looked round. Perhaps someone had knocked and left a parcel, but there was nothing on the benches either side of the porch, or even outside. Puzzled, she came back in and bolted the door again.

The interruption had distracted her from her book and she decided it was time to make herself a pot of tea. She walked into the kitchen and stopped, stock still, just inside the door. There was a man, a stranger, standing in the middle of the room.

At her gasp, he turned round. Her heart pounded violently as she realised he was the man she had seen wandering round the cottage weeks previously. The prowler. But Luke had said it was his brother so there was no need to be frightened of him.

"You must be Jason," she said, a little shakily. "I'm afraid Luke isn't here at the moment. If you were to come back this evening — "

"So you're the girl Luke took in. The one that's lost her memory." His eyes took her in from head to toe, an insolent expression on his face. "My God, he didn't waste much time, did he?"

His eyes were riveted on her stomach. Indignantly, she burst out, "But Luke isn't — " The explanation died on her lips. Jason stepped forward and grasped her arm, twisting her round to face him. He thrust his face close to hers.

"Let's have a look at you. Good-looker all right. Old Luke certainly knows how to pick 'em. And your memory is a complete blank, so he says?"

Carol looked up at the face above her. Then, with a blinding flash of clarity, realisation hit her like an ice-cold douche of water into her mind.

"You!" she gasped. "It was you! I remember your face! It was cloudy but I saw your face for a moment when the moon came out! Before — "

"You're the one who doesn't remember anything. You don't want to remember, so mind you keep it that way," he snarled, shaking her roughly.

"But I do remember!" Carol cried wildly. "You were there, in the wood — "

She felt a tremendous blow, like an explosion, strike the side of her head, as Jason's fist shot out and made contact with her left temple. She had the sensation of falling, but before she reached the floor, the whole world blackened out around her.

6

SHE woke screaming, and it was some minutes before she was aware that Luke was with her and that it was his voice, comforting and calm, speaking to her.

"Carol, my love, it's all right. You've had a nightmare but you're all right; nothing bad is going to happen to you." He took her hands, holding them between his own, seeking to transfer some of his tranquillity to her. Gradually the screams subsided to sobbing, and the violent shaking which had accompanied it slowed until she was shivering with the chill of the cold sweat which enveloped her.

"My poor darling; tell me all about it," Luke soothed. She leant against him, feeling that the only safety in the world belonged in his arms.

It took a long time before she could speak. Describing the nightmare meant that she relived it, and it was not until she was fully awake, fully convinced that Luke was with her, sitting on the side of the bed and holding her close, that she could bear to remember.

"I was in that wood. You know, just near the road where you found me. And then I thought there was someone following me. I began to hurry and I heard footsteps behind me, hurrying too. I ran — and he ran, and I tripped, and — he caught me."

"It was only a dream. You're awake now." Luke massaged her shoulders, where fear had tensed her muscles into rigid knots.

"Not, it wasn't a dream. It really happened."

"You were asleep. I looked in when I came home and you were sound asleep."

Carol looked at him and noticed for the first time that Luke was wearing his dressing-gown.

"What time is it?" she asked, frowning.

"About three in the morning," he yawned.

"*What?* What's happened? How did I get here?" She looked down at herself. Under the bed's duvet she was fully dressed.

"You were asleep on your bed when I came home, about seven, so I covered you over and left you to wake up. I did some work until about eleven, then I went to bed myself. I suppose I ought to have looked in on you again, but I didn't think of it."

"But I didn't go to sleep on my bed!" Carol exclaimed. "I was downstairs. I'd gone to make some tea and there he was — Luke, I was terrified! But I was in the kitchen, not here. Are you sure you didn't carry me upstairs?"

"Quite sure. I'd know if I'd carried you anywhere. You're no lightweight these days."

"But how did I get here? He hit me and I must have passed out." Carol raised a hand to her face and winced as she touched tender places on her cheek and nose.

"What are you talking about? Who is this 'he' you keep mentioning?"

"It was Jason, your brother. He was in the kitchen. He'd let himself into the cottage and he hit me."

"He what? Jason, here, you say? And he hit you?" Luke asked incredulously.

"He wanted to see you. I told him you were gone for the day." She stopped, confused. How was she going to tell Luke what she knew about his own brother?

"I blacked out. But that was in the kitchen," she ended.

"Carol, when I found you in bed asleep last night, you were breathing very heavily and there was a strong smell of whisky. Do you think you could have fallen and forgotten what happened?" Luke probed gently.

"Whisky? What do you mean? What are you saying?"

"There was an empty bottle and a

glass on the kitchen table. And quite a bit spilt, too."

"And you think I was drinking while you were out — you know I hate spirits of any kind!"

"I was puzzled, I admit. But you were so het up about the psychiatrist that I thought perhaps — "

"I never touched any alcohol. I would never have thought of doing anything like that," Carol said. "But you're right that there's a smell of it. It's on my clothes. But I didn't touch the bottle."

"I believe you. It certainly didn't seem like you. But what did happen yesterday? And what caused that terrible nightmare you had just now?"

"I remembered what happened," Carol said. "And I didn't want to face up to it. I don't even know if I can tell you now."

"Try to," Luke urged. "You must; it's the only way you'll ever be free of the past. I'm here with you; I won't let any harm come to you."

"Jason was here," Carol began. "I went

160

into the kitchen and found him there; he'd just walked in by himself. When I saw him properly, I remembered I'd seen him before."

"Where was that?"

"In that wood. I was walking there and he grabbed hold of me and I fought with him — "

"But that was in your dream," Luke broke in. "It was a nightmare, not real. You woke up screaming."

"No, it was real. I was reliving it in my dream, but it really did happen. It was Jason in that wood, and Luke, he raped me."

"He did *what*?"

"He raped me, Luke. He grabbed hold of me and pushed me down on the grass. Then he pulled up my skirt and raped me. That's why I was running blindly along the road and I didn't see your car. I was running away from him."

"Are you sure this really happened?"

"I'm really pregnant, aren't I? Luke, it happened. I'm not dreaming it and

I'm not lying to you. He raped me in the woods the night you knocked me down. I remember every detail clearly now."

"And are you saying it *was* Jason, or that Jason looked like this person, and so you remembered?"

"It was Jason. And he recognised me too, so he hit me. It knocked me out. Oh, Luke, I'm so sorry it had to turn out to be your brother!"

"I know Jason's a rake. He's a criminal and a lot of other things, but rape! I find it hard to believe that."

"I know I was having a nightmare, but I was remembering it all and it all really happened," Carol said. "I remember that wood. I had a peculiar feeling when I saw it again that time you drove me past the place where you found me. I think I might have remembered then, if I'd let myself. But I didn't want to. I shut it out of my mind and I wouldn't let myself remember."

"If Jason hit you and knocked you

162

out, I suppose he carried you up here and put you on the bed?"

"I suppose he must have done."

"And spilt whisky over you to make it look as if you were drunk?"

"I think he must have poured some down my throat. It feels terrible," Carol added. "And it's on my blouse — spilt down the front."

"The swine! And if he's touched you again — "

"No, Luke. He hasn't this time. I'm sure of it."

"Just let me get my hands on him, the rat!" Luke fumed. "He's done just about everything else that's criminal. I don't know why I should be surprised at this, too."

He put his arms round her. "My poor darling, what a ghastly experience! But at least, now we know what happened. There's no husband or lover wanting to take you away from me. And the baby — Jason's child — is my responsibility. Never fear for the future, Carol, my love. I'll take care of you and the baby, always. He's mine too, in a sense. When he's born, I'll adopt him legally and then he'll be safe. Jason's going to get the biggest thrashing of his life if he ever turns up here again. I'll see he leaves the district permanently. Does he realise, do you think — he must have seen that you were carrying, but do you think he realised he was responsible?"

"I don't know. I don't think so. Luke, I'll be all right if I don't ever have to face him again, or as long as you're there when I do. But I don't want this baby to be his. He's so — violent."

"It won't be his; it will be ours." Luke buried his face in her hair. "Environment and upbringing count for far more than heredity. And Jason is a one-off, he's exceptional. If heredity counted, he and I would be more alike, having the same father. It was our upbringing which made each of us what we are, so have no fears for the child. He'll grow up to be a good son, a credit to you."

"I may have a daughter," Carol smiled.

"Then she will grow up to be as beautiful and sweet as her mother." Luke kissed Carol's forehead; his lips trailed down to leave delicious, gentle kisses on each of her eyelids. She raised her arms round his neck, pulling him down towards her. Luke settled himself, lying on the bed beside her, one arm round her, holding her against him, the other caressing her tenderly.

"I feel so big and ungainly," Carol said, a little tremulously, "like a beached whale. And I suppose I shall go on getting even bigger right up to the end of September."

"You look beautiful to me," Luke told her. "You can have no idea what a relief I feel. I haven't forgotten that you had a terrible experience, so terrible that it affected your mind profoundly, but you've faced it at last and now it'll never have the power to frighten you again. You've remembered, so the nightmare's over. And it's over for me, too, now I know there's no other man."

"I told you I couldn't imagine loving anyone else but you," Carol said sleepily. She leaned against him. After the exhaustion of her nightmare, she was drowsy. "What did you say the time was?"

"Middle of the night. S'cold, too." She snuggled against him. "Luke, don't leave me."

He pulled the duvet round both of them and they lay, curled up together, sleeping peacefully until the sun's rays pierced the chinks in the curtain and shone fully on Luke's face.

He roused sleepily, easing a cramped arm from underneath Carol. She stirred and stretched out a hand towards him.

"Luke," she mumbled.

"I'm here. I have to move; I'm numb. But I'll be back." He kissed her lightly on her cheek, but she was already sound asleep again.

He tucked the duvet round her and tiptoed downstairs. It was nearly nine o'clock and she looked as if she would sleep on for at least another hour. He made himself a pot of tea and took it back upstairs to his desk.

Carol awoke gradually some time later and lay, listening to the familiar sound of Luke's tyepwriter, muffled through both closed doors. She savoured the sense of deep happiness and contentment; Luke had slept in her bed last night. There was still the indentation at the side of the pillow where his head had lain. She had had a nightmare and he had come to comfort her and stayed. She remembered that nightmare. Jason had triggered the memory, forced her to face and relive those hours of horror, when she had struggled with him in the wood, realising his strength was far greater than hers and he could do with her whatever he wanted. She had not expected to survive. His violence had convinced her that when he was finished with her, he would kill her. But then, incredibly, there had been a moment when his attention had been distracted and she had seized her chance. It must have been completely instinctive, for her mind and body were so dulled by pain and fear by then that she doubted she would have been capable of conscious thought. Something had made her scramble to her feet and run, finding the way in the darkness through that wood. Something had guided her, for normally she must have stumbled over brambled and tree roots, as she could hear Jason doing as he blundered after her.

She had run straight through the field, unerringly towards the stile leading on to the road, though she hadn't known it was there. Jason must have stopped chasing her before then, for he hadn't been on the road or Luke would have seen him. She had still been running, too terrified to stop, until Luke's car had come round the bend and the full headlights had dazzled her. All she had felt was a tremendous blow on her side as the car's wing struck her, spinning her round and hurling her on to the roadway. After that, nothing; until she had woken up in the hospital.

Glancing at her bedside clock, Carol saw it was past ten. Bright sunlight streamed through the curtains, indicating a warm day. She threw back the duvet and reached for her dressing-gown, then noticed that she was still fully dressed. She shuddered, remembering how she must have been carried upstairs by Jason, helplessly unconscious. Perhaps her pregnant state had put him off, because otherwise it was surprising he hand't taken advantage of her yet again.

Luke heard her open her door and called to her.

"Do you feel better now?"

"I'm not frightened any more. But my face — " She put her hand up to her cheek as the act of speaking caused a painful spasm.

"You've got a hefty bruise there! That's another score I have to settle with Jason." Luke went downstairs with her and took her to the window to examine her face in the light.

"Hmmm. No serious damage, but quite a swelling," he remarked. "Think you can manage to eat anything?"

Carol shook her head. "Maybe warm porridge. I couldn't cope with anything else. The bruise has stiffened since last night."

Luke made some gruel which Carol ate with some discomfort. Afterwards, he said, "I'm going to seek out Jason and have a showdown with him. He's forfeited any right to help from me now. I was going to try to keep him out of prison, but he's better inside, and for a long time, too."

"Luke, be careful. And please don't leave me alone. He might come here again."

"That's not likely. I know where to find him and I'll go straight there. It suddenly came to me this morning — there was a news broadcast some time ago, about a young woman being attacked round here. The police were

170

looking for a man but no more was mentioned so presumably they didn't arrest anyone. It could well have been Jason. He's got to be stopped, and, brother or not, I'm going to have to stop him."

"Would I have to give evidence in court, if he's arrested?" Carol asked.

"If he's attacked others, it might not be necessary to call you as witness. But he's got to be stopped. Neither you nor any other woman will be safe until he's in custody."

"I would be prepared to identify him as the man who raped me," Carol said. "Though, with my history of loss of memory, I doubt if they would trust my evidence."

"I'll go at once and find him. He'll be expecting to hear from me, as I said I'd try to make arrangements for a job for him. I thought he'd make a new start if I could find him work somewhere where he'd not have opportunity for theft, somewhere away from his old cronies. But this changes everything!

There's no place anywhere for him now."

"You're sure he won't turn up here while you're out?"

"I'm as certain as I can be. But stay inside and bolt everywhere. Don't open for anyone, till I get back."

"It was early afternoon before Carol heard the sound of Luke's car returning up the lane. She couldn't read the expression on his face as he came up the path, but, seeing that he was alone, she ran out to meet him.

"Jason confirmed your story," he said grimly. "In fact, he embellished it. Not only did he admit to everything, the scoundrel sounded quite proud of it. He even bragged about a couple of other girls he'd molested in March. The man's a menace; I've done with helping him, for ever. He'll stand trial and there shouldn't be the slightest doubt of a conviction." Luke walked into the living-room and flung himself into his usual easy chair.

"Get me a drink, will you? A stiff

172

whisky, please." He passed a hand over his eyes, reaching out blindly for the glass she brought him. Carol pushed it into his hands, hesitating by the chair, not knowing whether it was better to leave him alone or if he wanted her to stay.

"Jason was — is — the only close relative I have," he said, talking almost to himself. "I don't ever feel I had anything in common with him, but we shared a father and that was something I shared with no one else in the world. It's a certainty he'll be put away for years and I had to be the one to do it. I could have helped him get right away. He asked me to. I could have bought him an air ticket to somewhere beyond the reach of the law, somewhere where perhaps he could have made good. He promised me he'd put all his crimes behind him if only I'd help him this last time." Luke gave a shuddering sob. "And I walked into the first police station I passed on my way back, and told them everything.

They'll be arriving at his hideout about now, where's he's waiting for me to come back with his ticket and some money."

Carol could find no words of comfort to offer. There was nothing to be said so she put her arms tightly round Luke and rested her head against his shoulder.

"Poor Luke! You comforted me when I had no one. If only I could comfort you," she murmured.

"At least, I have you. Sorry, little one, for wallowing in a load of self-pity. It was a harrowing morning but I'm over it now. How about finding me something to eat? I didn't have time for any lunch and I'm starving."

He followed her out to the kitchen and stood leaning against the door while Carol set about preparing some salad and cold meat.

"We've three months at the outside," he said unexpectedly.

"Three months? What for?" Carol looked up from laying the table.

"Three months before your baby is due. I think we should make plans to be married as soon as possible. We don't need to delay and we should be properly wed before he's born."

"Luke!" She gazed at him with eyes wide with amazement.

He took the cutlery from her hands and laid it down on the table before taking her in his arms.

"It's an unromantic proposal, I'm afraid. Blame it on my heroes all being strong, silent types. But now I'm sure the baby is Jason's this is at least one thing I can do for him, though he won't appreciate it. Will you settle for a quiet wedding at the local register office in, say, about three weeks' time?"

"Luke, I'd settle for anything!"

His kiss was a real one, not the affectionate but brotherly gestures she had grown to accept. She clung to him, as close as the swelling bulk of her abdomen would let her.

They discussed plans over lunch.

"Tomorrow I'll drive into town and

visit the Registrar," Luke said. "I'll need — damn! I'd forgotten. I'll need your birth certificate."

Carol sat very still.

"I suppose I could get a copy of it. Only — your name isn't — really — Carol Legat, is it? I'd forgotten. What is it really?"

"I don't know. I can't remember," Carol said dully.

Luke looked at her hard. "You remembered walking in the wood when Jason found you. But what were you doing in the wood? Where had you come from?"

"I don't know. I tell you, I can't remember. I only remembered about Jason when I saw him," Carol repeated.

"But you must remember! You can't have just part of your memory come back and the rest stay blank," Luke protested.

"I don't remember anything before the wood. I'm sorry, Luke."

"Then we must help you to remember. I'm not thinking straight in forgetting that there was more to it than you being attacked by Jason."

"Please, Luke. It was bad enough remembering about that. Let's leave it for now," Carol begged.

"But we can't get married without your knowing who you are. You must see that," Luke said. "Look, confronting Jason brought that part back, so we must do the same again. We'll go back to the wood, try to retrace your steps, find out where you came from. Whyever didn't I insist that we did this before? We'll go back and back — "

"*No!*" Carol gripped the table top so tightly that her knuckles showed white.

"You'll be perfectly safe. No more harm can possibly come to you. I'll be with you every step of the way."

"I can't! Don't make me!"

Luke came round to her side of the table and put both hands on her shoulders, forcing her to look into his face.

"Carol — you do remember, don't

you?" he said very quietly.

"No! I don't want to remember! I can't! I don't!" she cried wildly.

"You must! Whatever it is, you have to face it!" His grip on her shoulders tightened and he shook her slightly. "Don't you see, there can be no future for you, no peace, no anything until you face up to whatever it is in your past."

"Leave me alone, Luke. You don't understand," she muttered.

His face hardened. "I've had just about enough of this pretence. You've *got* to remember. I'll make you."

"You can't make me."

He looked at her as if he was seeing her for the first time. "I think you remembered all the time," he said. "I think it has all been pretence."

"No!"

"There must be something! You must have something with you that would give us a clue!" He frowned in thought, then said, "You handbag — there must be something we've missed in it. You

178

must have *something* in it that would identify you."

"There's nothing in it," she denied.

"Bring it to me here."

"But there's nothing — "

"It's over there, lying by the stairs in the hall. Bring it to me," he commanded.

Luke watched her as she took the half dozen paces into the hall and picked up the leather handbag. Silently she handed it to him. He pulled back the zip and tipped the contents out on to the table amid the remains of their meal. There were several extra items she had acquired since leaving hospital and he picked these out, moving them to one side. He picked out the latchkey with the shamrock ring and weighed it in his hand consideringly.

"If I were to ask you what door this unlocked, could I guess at the answer I'd get?" he asked.

Carol made no reply.

Luke put the key down and picked up the coin purse.

"I told you. They're all meaningless. Just things. Ordinary, commonplace bits and pieces that any woman carried around in her bag," she insisted.

"Your clothes — the ones you were wearing that night?" he demanded.

"I threw them away. They aren't any use now."

"Why not?"

"Well, for one thing, they don't fit any more. And they weren't mine anyway." She stopped, her breath sucked in sharply. She stood very still.

"What do you mean, they weren't yours?"

"They somehow didn't seem my style. They weren't at all my taste in clothes. I don't know why I was wearing them. Perhaps the hospital made a mistake. After all, when I came to, I was wearing a hospital nightgown. They told me they were my clothes but they might have mixed them up with another patient."

"Do you really think so?" There was a harshness in Luke's tone which

180

frightened her. She took refuge in silence.

Luke picked up the empty handbag, plunging his hand into it, as she had once done. And, like her, his fingers touched something hard beneath the lining.

"What's this?"

He ripped apart the lining and picked out the diamond ring. He held out his hand; the stone, sparkling up at them, lay on his palm between them.

"This looks to me very much like someone's engagement ring," Luke said very slowly. "How did it come to be in your handbag, Carol?"

"I don't know. I've told you, these things may not even be mine. The hospital said — "

"The bag *is* yours. This ring is yours too, isn't it?"

"I don't remember. I don't know."

"That's always your excuse, isn't it, Carol? I think you *do* remember! I think you've remembered for a very long time now, and you won't admit it.

perhaps you never lost your memory at all. Perhaps it was all a ploy to conceal who you really are and what you're running away from." Luke's voice was cold with anger. "Was that what really happened, Carol? Have you been lying all this time?"

"Please, Luke," she sobbed. "I can't bear it when you're angry. I never meant to deceive you or anyone. I didn't want to remember. I tried to shut the past out of my mind, to pretend none of it happened, and then I couldn't remember. I really couldn't."

"You've faced up to Jason. There's no more to fear. You *can* remember now. He has no more power to harm you. All that is over and it can't happen to you again." Luke spoke more gently but there was a firmness in the set of his mouth; a determination to have answers, which frightened her.

"It's not Jason," she whispered. "There are other things. I can't talk about it."

"This ring? It is an engagement ring,

isn't it? And it's yours. So there *is* a man in your forgotten past, after all. Why he hasn't come forward is still a mystery, but he exists, that's for sure. And if he gave you an engagement ring, why not a wedding-ring, too? Are you married, Carol? Perhaps there's a husband back in your past. Perhaps you were pregnant *before* you went walking in that wood. Perhaps Jason isn't the father of your baby, even though he's admitted to raping you. Is that the real truth, Carol!"

"No! No!" She covered her face with her hands, trying to shut out the probing questions, and Luke's anger.

"I want answers. Truthful answers. You've been deceiving me for long enough," he said sternly.

"I haven't deceived you. Truly, I couldn't remember. I shut everything out of my mind."

"Exactly what do you remember, or not remember? I want to know the whole truth."

"I only remember that the situation

was so intolerable I ran away. I wanted to forget everything and everyone. The night you found me, the real me disappeared and by chance, Carol Legat came into existence in the hospital."

"But this ring. You knew about this ring?"

Miserably she nodded. "Yes, I know about the ring. I found it under the lining of my bag soon after I came here."

"Why didn't you tell me then? You must have known it would be a vital clue in tracing your family."

"I didn't want to."

"I can see that! You haven't wanted to remember or trace anyone, from the beginning. You've resisted everyone's efforts to help you remember. Were you also afraid that hypnosis would show that you did remember, after all? And would it have revealed secrets you'd rather no one knew?"

Carol didn't answer. Luke, controlling his anger, asked, "Who are you really?

184

You know, don't you? I think you've always known."

"My name is Carol Legat."

Luke exploded. "Carol Legat was the name you acquired in error at the hospital. You know that as well as I do! Listen to me. You can't keep up this pretence for ever. There'll be countless problems mounting up, the longer this goes on. You have to stop running away. You have to face up to your past and conquer it. It's the only way you can be free of it."

"Leave me alone, Luke. I can't take any more." She sat down at the table, mildly surprised to see the remains of their meal still lying there. Had it really been only a short while ago that she and Luke had been discussing wedding plans?

"Very well, Carol. I'll leave you alone. I'm going out now. I've things to do — and I may be away some time. I'm giving you a chance to think about what I've said and when I get back I shall expect you to tell me exactly who you are and where you've come from, and who this man is — " He gestured towards the ring. "I *know* you can remember everything if you want to, so no more of this pretence. Is that understood?"

He strode out of the kitchen and took the stairs two at a time. Carol heard him opening cupboards and drawers in his bedroom, then, a few minutes later, he reappeared, carrying his briefcase and a holdall.

"You're staying away overnight?" Her heart sank.

"I'm going to London. I'll probably stay with my publisher. You'll be quite safe here, Jason must be in custody by now."

"Luke — don't leave me!"

"What's the point in my staying? I was crazy enough to imagine we could get married. It was an impossible idea. You probably are married already — at least you have a fiancé, and your baby already has a father."

"Was that the only reason you were

going to marry me?" she whispered.

Luke looked at her for a long moment. "Wasn't that what you wanted?" he said harshly. "You knew I'd feel responsible for Jason's child."

"Luke — "

He turned away, striding out through the back door, down the path to the car.

Carol watched him go; a cold, numb feeling where her heart had been. Did he really believe she had used him, had only wanted him as a means of escape, to provide a father and security for her child? And how was she to prove otherwise, convince him that she loved only him and that in spite of all the evidence, there had never been anyone else but Luke, ever?

7

FOR a long time after Luke had gone, Carol sat staring into space. She wasn't aware of her surroundings, of anything. Her thoughts were miles away, following paths she had not dared pursue.

Eventually she roused herself and stood up. There was only one course open to her now. To go back; follow the trail back every step until she had faced the whole truth about herself and her past.

She went upstairs and borrowed a small suitcase from Luke's room. She packed a few clothes, enough for a few days but still light enough for her to carry.

It was seven or eight miles to the place where she had run into Luke's car on that fateful night; much too far to walk, especially in her condition.

On top of the bookcase in the living-room she found a bus timetable and looked up the routes. If she went into town, then out again on a different bus, it would bring her to within a short distance of the wood. Quickly she checked times. It could be done that afternoon if she was lucky and there were no delays. Carol pushed the timetable into her handbag.

The final thing she now had to do was to check how much money she had. Luke paid her generous wages which she usually banked, since there hadn't been much opportunity to spend, but there was a jam jar at the back of her drawer, full of notes and loose change, that had lain there, untouched, for some time. She had wanted to pay him back for the clothes he had bought her when she first left hospital, and when he had laughingly refused, saying he could well afford them, and she could count it as part of the job, she had put the money aside with some idea of buying him a present when she had the opportunity.

She counted it out, spreading coins and notes over the bed. To her surprise and relief, there was quite a sizeable sum, nearly a hundred pounds. She scooped it up, adding it to her now bulging handbag.

Carol gave a last look back as she opened the gate leading to the lane. The cottage was as she had first seen it, in Luke's photo, which he had shown her when she had been in the hospital; roses and honeysuckle entwined, climbing over the porch and round the upper windows. The garden was full of old-fashioned, country flowers, their perfume coming to her on the balmy sunny air. She had a strong feeling that she might never see the cottage again, and she stayed for a long moment memorising the scene. When she had first come here, there had been snow covering everything. How long ago that seemed now!

At last she turned away and the lingering fragrance of the garden was the memory she knew would stay with her forever. Whatever tricks her memory might play on her in the future, Carol knew that the scent of roses, lavender and carnations would evoke bitter-sweet thoughts; that whenever she saw a country garden such as this, she would always, to the end of her life, remember the happiest days she had ever known.

She was weary by the time she had walked to the bus-stop and stood waiting for twenty minutes for the bus into town. The journey gave her a chance to rest, however, and there was only a brief wait at the bus-station for the second bus out again. She felt very alone when she stepped off at the crossroads near to the wood. As the bus drew away she resisted an urge to call after it to stop and let her on again, to be driven away from this lonely spot.

It was about five hundred yards from the crossroads to the place where Luke had brought her. When she recognised it, she began looking for the gap in the hedge where the stile had been. Just fifty yards or so further and she came upon it, with its path along the edge of the field leading directly to the wood.

It wasn't easy to climb the stile with her ungainly body, carrying the suitcase and her handbag. It was at this point that the baby started kicking violently and she had to stop and rest for several minutes until things subsided again.

The field had a crop of corn, breast high now. She wouldn't have remembered the path, for it had been the middle of winter when she had run along it in the opposite direction.

Must have run along it. She genuinely didn't remember and only the knowledge that she must have come from the wood, directed her steps towards it. Only a sense of uneasiness and growing nervousness told her that her instinct was leading her in the right direction. What would happen after she reached the wood, she didn't know.

The wood was larger than it had appeared from the road. It dipped into a hollow and on entering it, she followed a well-used track downwards for some distance.

The track brought her to a glade, an attractive, grassy spot ringed with trees and thick, bushy vegetation. In other circumstances it would have suggested at once the ideal place for a family picnic. There was even a large, flat stone in the centre. She went over to it and knew at once that here was the place where Jason had caught her. There was even the tree stump and a tangle of roots where she had tripped as she ran away from him.

She looked for some track or path, leading away from the clearing. There was a faint, worn line in the grass and she followed it to the far edge, where the trees and bushes began again. Sure enough, there was a gap with a path leading back into the wood. She wasn't sure whether this was the right direction to take. At this time she wasn't sure of anything. All paths in the wood looked alike, but she followed the track away from the glade, following the same general direction.

It ended at a fence with a lane beside it. Without hesitation, she turned left and followed the lane until she came to another stile that led into a field. She was not even thinking which way now; instinctively she was retracing the route she had taken, knowing she had come this way.

The field sloped upwards, and as she came to the brow of the hill, she saw a small farmhouse nestling in a hollow, with a cart track leading away across the fields. It looked remote, no road or other dwelling in sight.

Carol walked up through the farmyard, inches deep in mud which had dried now to rock-hard ruts. It had been a sea of mire in January. She didn't hesitate until she came up to the back door of the house and knocked loudly on it. Then, all at once, her courage deserted her. What on earth am I doing here, she thought. However am I going to explain myself?

The farmer's wife, a plump woman

in her thirties, opened the door. Carol said the first thing that came into her head.

"Do you do bed and breakfast accommodation?"

"I do. What would you be wanting — a single? For tonight? It's rather short notice. I haven't a room ready."

"How many rooms do you have?"

"Only the one single, and a double that could be a family room. I couldn't offer you that — I might have an enquiry for a double later."

"That's all right. But may I see the single room, please?" Carol asked.

"Certainly, madam. You'll have to excuse it not being cleaned up. I don't often get asked for a single, so it's shut up most of the time." She stepped back to allow Carol to enter the huge farm kitchen. Were all kitchens alike in the country, Carol wondered. It looked like a larger version of the one at the cottage and she couldn't decide whether that was the reason it seemed familiar, or if it was because she had been here before.

The farmer's wife took her upstairs and opened a door leading off a dark landing. The room was very small but spotlessly clean. Even the linoleum shone from an energetic polishing.

"I can have it ready in an hour," the woman said. "Do you want to leave your luggage, or will you pay me a deposit?"

Carol could not bring herself to step on to the gleaming floor, afraid of making footmarks, but she stared round at the bed, the washbasin in the corner, the cheap wooden cupboard and chest, the home-made rag rug on the floor by the bed. She was quite sure she had never seen this room before.

"It's a very nice room," she said, "but I'm not sure that I'll be staying. You see — "

"Laura!" a man's voice bellowed from below.

"My husband. You must excuse me. We've got a sick calf and everything's chaotic today." She hurried downstairs and Carol followed her.

"Who was that?" Carol heard the farmer asking.

"Oh, just a lady come about a room. I was showing her the single."

"Didn't see her car. Look, the vet says — " he broke off as Carol appeared down the stairs.

"Good afternoon, madam. Excuse me, won't you, but we've problems with the herd. Vet says he'll prescribe some medicine, and give her an injection now. He'll come back tomorrow to see how she is." Having delivered his message, he turned to go outside, then paused, staring at Carol.

"I know you, don't I, ma'am? You've stayed here before, I think."

"Really? Do you remember me?" Carol asked.

"Never forget a face. We don't have too many new ones round these parts, that's why." He laughed, a big, hearty guffaw at himself.

"I think I've stayed here before. But I'm not really sure. You see, I had an accident and lost my memory. I'm trying to trace my movements back to that night," Carol explained.

"Lost your memory! You poor soul! come into the kitchen; I was about to make some tea. Perhaps John can help you. He's got a wonderful memory for folk." Laura took in Carol's condition at a glance, and shepherded her towards an easy chair by the fireplace. A huge Aga filled the alcove, with a kettle singing on top of it.

"Tell us all about it," Laura said, bustling about fetching cups and the teapot.

John, the farmer, settled himself at the table, where he could see Carol. "'Bout a year ago," he said thoughtfully. "No, not as much as that. Christmas time, or a little after."

"That's right. It was the first week in January I was taken into hospital. It was then."

"You didn't stay here," John said. "We wouldn't have had paying guests that time of year. Season ends by October, latest."

198

"I remember!" There was a clatter and Laura nearly dropped the milk jug in her excitement. "You came knocking at the door one afternoon, about four or five. It was dark and raining, and you looked done-in, poor lass. You were soaking wet, too. You'd fallen in the muck getting through the yard. You were in a terrible state! My, I didn't know that was you!"

"I remember going along a dark track and then seeing lights. The only lights I'd seen for ages," Carol said.

"We're the only farm near here. Pitch black outside it is, at night. Our lights would have been the only ones you'd see. No wonder you came to us."

"But why did I come here?" Carol asked. "I've tried to shut the memory of all this out of my mind for so long, I've actually succeeded and now I really don't know. I need all the information you can give me. I've got to find out everything — why I came here, every detail."

"I remember that night well, now

I look at you," Laura said, pouring steaming cups of tea. "I thought you were some sort of apparition! You asked for a room, but in the end you didn't stay. I hadn't the heart to refuse, even though we don't reckon to take people in the winter. You were wet through, and the little bag you had with you was all soggy, with all your things spoilt, so I found you something to wear while you had a hot bath. Terrible state you were in."

"You — found me something to wear?" Carol couldn't help looking at the farmer's wife, at least six inches taller and several sizes larger than herself. Laura interpreted the look and laughed. "They weren't my things," she said. "They weren't anything special, but at least they were clean and dry." She looked embarrassed. "I sorted out a reasonable skirt, a blouse and cardigan from a sackful of clothes we'd been collecting for a jumble sale. I wasn't expecting you to be needing them for long, just till I could dry your own things and clean 'em up a bit."

"But you said I didn't stay after all?"

"You were that jumpy — anybody'd think a pack of hounds were after you," John said.

"You had a hot bath, and changed into the dry clothes — "

"Where did the clothes come from?" Carol interrupted.

"Heavens, I don't know! Anywhere, they might have. But those I picked out for you were clean and good, even if they did look a bit frumpish. Someone's old school uniform, I remember thinking at the time. But it wasn't too obviously schoolish, if you know what I mean."

"There was a nametape on the cardigan," Carol said. "Carol Legat."

"Really? I suppose that must be who they belonged to, once. Name doesn't mean anything," Laura shrugged dismissively.

"They found the nametape when they took the cardigan off me in hospital," Carol said. "They thought that was my name."

"Natural, I suppose. But then you told them — "

"No. I let them call me that. At the time I'd forgotten about the clothes not being mine, and when I first regained consciousness I really didn't know who I was or where I was, for a time."

"You never told us your name, either," John said. "As I recall, you were too busy being fussed over by Laura. We've thought of you often, since. The half-drowned young lady we called you."

"The hospital authorities tried to trace my relatives through a news item on TV, but no one came forward," Carol said.

"There now! We'd have spoken up if we'd known, but we don't have a TV," Laura told her. "We rarely have the time to watch, and reception is poor here; we're in a hollow, see, with hills round about."

"You said I didn't stay here. But what then did I do? Where did I stay?"

"That's something we've wondered

ourselves," John said. "The wife here had made you some hot soup and you came down from the bathroom in those clothes — funny you looked, and very different from the sort of things you'd been wearing."

"I'd put the food on the table," Laura took up the tale, "but you were so jumpy, like as if you thought something — or someone — was chasing after you. You sat by the fire but you couldn't keep still, you were that nervous. About half past nine, you suddenly said you were going out for a walk. It'd stopped raining by then, or we'd have been firmer against it. You were in no fit state to go wandering about at night. Besides, there's nowhere to go round here."

"But you went, all the same," John said. "And that was the last we ever saw of you."

"I suppose we should have got the police," Laura said. "But we didn't. I thought you'd not fancied staying with us after all. John thought you were running away from home. Truth is, I was afraid bringing the police in might have caused trouble for you. You were clearly frightened of something or someone coming after you, but I couldn't believe it was anything bad you might have done."

"You said I had a bag with me? You don't still have it, I suppose?" Carol asked.

"Yes, it's still here. I had a feeling you'd come back one day, though John never thought so."

"We both thought you were running away. I thought it was from your parents, but Laura said these days girls don't run away, they walk out. Don't seem much difference to me. I thought maybe you'd changed your mind and gone back. Least said, soonest mended. That's why we didn't get in touch with the police. We figured it was your business, after all."

"Here's your bag." Laura had gone to a cupboard under the stairs and now she brought out a small canvas holdall, water-stained and marked with mould. With nervous fingers Carol tugged at the zip, then tipped the contents on to the hearthrug in front of her.

The clothes were crumpled and traces of mildew where they'd been damp, clung to them. They were smart, expensive, trendy clothes, quite different from those she had been wearing when Luke's car had knocked her down. She knew at once that these were the kind of clothes she would have chosen for herself; they were her style though rather younger than the clothes she might buy these days.

"Was there nothing else?" She turned the clothes over. There must be something other than merely clothes.

"Your sponge-bag. You left it in the bathroom. It's still there, in the cupboard," Laura said.

"But no papers — nothing personal — no identification?" Carol ran her hand round the inside of the now empty bag.

"To be frank with you, I never

looked," Laura confessed. "It felt a bit like prying. John said I ought to, so that at least we could let someone know the bag was here. But I was sure you'd come back for it. I put it away in the cupboard and after a few days I forgot all about it."

Carol picked up the bag and then she noticed it had an outside zipped pocket. She pulled it open; inside she could hear the crackle of paper. She spread the contents on the floor beside her. There was the counterfoil of a steamship ticket, Dublin to Holyhead, with the date 6th January stamped on it, and there was an envelope, too, addressed to Miss Claire Graham, at an address in Dublin.

Carol stared at the envelope. The name sounded at first like that of someone she had once known, years ago, but could not put a face to. After so many months of answering to Carol Legat, the name Claire Graham was strange, like a maiden name after years of marriage. It was her own name and she knew it, and the address was familiar, too. It conjured at once the memories she had wanted to forget, memories she had pushed out of her mind for so long that she had almost succeeded in genuinely forgetting. Almost, but not quite.

The letter was trivial, an acknowledgement of an order for a magazine. Carol remembered picking it up from behind the front door as she left the Dublin house that day, carrying with her the overnight bag, a single ticket to England and a determination never to return. But she was going to have to return, wasn't she? Return to face and conquer the ghosts that haunted her from the past. And, because she had deceived Luke, she would have to face them alone.

"I'd like to stay here tonight after all, if that's convenient," Carol told Laura. "And I owe you an explanation as well as the cost of the room I took, even if I didn't stay. I've more money now than I had when I was here last."

"You paid me for the room in advance," Laura said. "That's why I was so sure you weren't wanted by the police. John said that wasn't logical, but I had an instinct about you."

Carol told them then, as far as she was able, what had happened to her after she had gone for that fateful walk in the dark. What she found difficult to explain to them was the feeling of fear she had had, while she had been at the farm, of the necessity not to stop in one place; to put as much distance between herself and her past as possible, even though she was tired and exhausted already.

She had left the farm some time after nine o'clock. The torrential rain had stopped and the night was clear. A moon had risen and it had been pleasant to walk along the silent lane, quite alone, away from Laura's well-meant fussing. She had needed to be alone to think what she should do next. She had wandered across the field, found the stile and then followed the lane until she found herself in the wood.

She'd always loved woods. The trees, rustling in the wind, made a comforting sound. There had been woods where she had come from, and she had found peace of mind on many occasions in the past, walking by herself under the leafy canopy.

But this wood was not peaceful for long. Soon, she realised she was no longer alone. The natural night rustlings of small animals had been too loud, too persistent. And then Jason Mackenzie had seen her. He had been living rough after having broken into a house a few miles away. He'd been released from a six months' prison sentence, barely a week previously, and Carol was the first woman he had seen in a situation where she was alone and vulnerable. She had been his for the taking, and, sex-starved and desperate, he had taken her.

It must have lasted a long time, Carol thought with a shudder. Nearly two hours of something so horrible, her mind had tried to shut it out, and had succeeded for a time at least.

"You poor thing!" Laura exclaimed, horrified. "Didn't you report him to the police? A beast like that shouldn't have been allowed to go free."

"When I woke up in hospital I didn't remember anything," Carol explained. "I had a broken leg; the hospital had no reason to look for anything but car injuries."

"How did you first come to our farm?" John wanted to know.

"I hitched-hiked. I remember, I walked off the ferry and made my way out to the main road. There were lorries and cars coming past continuously, and when a freight lorry stopped, I begged a lift. It was chance he was coming this way. I'd have taken any direction, so long as it was going away from the coast."

"You didn't come all that far. Most of those lorries off the steamer are long-distance."

"He stopped at a café along the road,

but I wanted to keep going so I tried to hitch another lift. It wasn't so easy as it was beginning to get dark by then. I tried walking but I got lost. I saw your lights in the distance so I walked towards them, through the fields. I thought if I tried to find a track or a road I'd lose sight of them and I'd never find anyone. I fell several times, and tore my clothes on barbed wire. I think I was wearing this." Carol held up a skirt, pretty but its hem in tatters and still stained with mud. "It was bucketing down with rain by then. I must have looked a terrible sight when I knocked on your door."

"You certainly did," Laura smiled. "I remember wondering what on earth had happened to you."

"You were so kind," Carol said. "I remember you sat me by the fire and gave me some brandy. I was shivering so much the glass kept rattling against my teeth."

"And you say a car knocked you down after you were attacked in the wood? And you've been living with the driver of it ever since?" John asked. Put like that, her story gave quite the wrong impression. Carol hastened to explain about Luke, though she did not mention Jason being his brother.

"And this Mr Mackenzie turns out to be Gerald Williams, the famous author!" Laura said. "How romantic! John and I are great fans of his. We've several of his books."

"Luke and I might have married," Carol said, and it was hard to keep the wistfulness out of her voice. "But he is convinced I may be married already. That's why I have to go back to Ireland — I'm not really sure myself if I'm truly free. I have to sort out my past."

"Couldn't he go with you?" Laura asked.

"Luke doesn't know I've gone. He was angry because I said I didn't remember — I didn't *want* to remember why I left Ireland. And it may be that I won't be able to come back. I don't know what I'll find when I get there."

"Tonight you must have a good rest," Laura said in her motherly way. "Tomorrow John's going into town to market — he'll drop you at the station and you can pick up the train to Holyhead. They'll tell you there the times of the boats. I wish you every success in solving all your problems."

"Carol was touched by the kindness of the couple. She spent the rest of the evening sharing supper with them, answering Laura's eager questions about Luke and his novels as best she could. Later, while John was outside, making a last round of the farmyard, Laura said, "Why don't you telephone Luke now, and let him know where you are? Surely he'll be worried about you."

"He's in London. He said he would probably stay with his publisher and I don't know where that is. When he comes back he'll understand why I've gone and that I can't come back until I've made some proper order of my life." She hadn't told Laura or John about the angry quarrel she and

Luke had had, and that he probably wouldn't want to hear from her because he believed she had returned to her husband, or at least, her fiancé.

"I'll write to him from Ireland," she said, to satisfy Laura, but she knew she wouldn't. She doubted if Luke would want to hear from her again.

The next morning John took her to the station, and by midday she had arrived in Holyhead. There was an overnight boat leaving that evening and by nightfall Carol was well on her way, back to the problems she had left behind, all those months ago.

8

THE boat docked at Dun Laoghaire early next morning. Customs formalities took very little time, since Carol had only two small holdalls with her, the one she had packed at the cottage, and the one Laura had returned to her. They had made an attempt to clean and iron the clothes in that one, but Carol hadn't wanted them anyway. Apart from the fact that they no longer fitted, they were yet another reminder of her past. She was a different person now, not only different in name, but far more confident and determined.

She found herself a taxi and gave the driver an address. Once he joined the traffic leaving the dock she knew there was no turning back, no chance of changing her mind.

It was a long ride, but at last the taxi pulled up outside a large, Georgian house on the outskirts of Dublin. She paid the man and he offered to carry her bags up the steps to the front door.

"No, I can manage, thanks." She wanted him gone before anyone saw her, yet she had the urge to ask him to stay. Once he had driven away there would be no one to turn for help, if she needed it.

"Sure, missus, I can't be leaving you with both them bags to carry up the stairs." He brushed aside her protests and picked up both holdalls in one hand, leaping up the steps to deposit them in front of the door.

"Will I ring for you?" He raised his hand to the doorbell.

"No!" Carol hurried after him. "I have a key," she explained.

The driver touched his cap in a courteous, old-fashioned gesture, and, jumping into his cab, drove off.

Carol fumbled in her handbag and drew out the key with the shamrock keyring. She fitted it in the lock and it turned easily. She pushed the door open and stepped over the threshold into the long, high-ceilinged entrance hall.

Memory flooded back, and with it the sense of fear. When she had last stood in this house, she had been terrified.

"But I'm not frightened now," Carol said aloud.

There was a sound to her left, from behind a closed door. Carol stiffened.

"Who's there?" a man's voice called. The door opened and a grey-haired man in his sixties came out into the hall. He stood quite still, staring at Carol for some moments in silence, then he said, "So! You've finally decided to come back. I always knew you would."

"I've come back because I've made decisions of my own," Carol said, striving to keep her voice steady.

"You've come to your senses at last. And not before time. Now perhaps you'll have learnt to do what you're bidden," he replied.

"I was in a car accident — and I lost my memory. It's a long story. May I come into your study and sit down?" Carol asked.

"Lost your memory! Well, that's a fancy excuse, I must say! I suppose I'd better hear whatever rubbish you've dreamed up."

He stepped back into the room, but as Carol made to follow him, he noticed her swollen figure and stepped back a pace in shock.

"What's this? Good God, don't tell me you're pregnant!"

"Yes, I am. I'll tell you about it — "

"You slut!" He swung his hand and the full force of it struck her across her face. "How dare you come back here in that condition, flaunting your shame! You deserve the thrashing of your life, my girl!"

"I was raped," Carol whispered, the tears smarting behind her eyes as the pain of the blow seared her cheek.

"Don't give me that! I likely story, I must say! You run off without a word; we don't hear anything of you for months and then back you come, in a shameful condition, expecting me to take you in — "

"I don't expect you to take me in," Carol said. "In fact, I've come back to tell you. I've made a new life for myself — " Her voice wavered as she remembered Luke storming out of the cottage; was that new life over for her now? She pressed on, determined to stand up for herself at last, against this man who had bullied her all her life.

"I'm free of this place and you and I'm going to stay that way. There's nothing you can force me to do now."

"Is there not? Do you think I'm going to stand for a daughter of mine bringing shame on her father's name — running off on the eve of her wedding — and now coming back, as bold as brass — in that condition?"

He had closed the door and to Carol's dismay, placed himself between her and it. She moved across the room and sat down on a small fireside chair. If she hadn't, she thought her legs would have given way under her.

She studied the man glaring at her across the room; Michael Graham, her father and a man she had feared and obeyed for as long as she could remember. He had bullied her mother, too, right up to the day of her death. Carol would never forgive him for that. They had been living in London then, but after his wife's death he had taken her to Dublin. He had said they were starting a new life; he was going into business with a wealthy partner. Carol had been sixteen then, and it wasn't until five years later, when the business began to founder, that she learnt that part of the conditions of the partnership had been that she should be promised in marriage to Ewan O'Hara.

She had always disliked Ewan. Uriah Heep, she called him to herself. He fawned over her, flattered her with embarrassing false compliments and couldn't pass by her without touching her. She had been appalled when he proposed, then horrified when her father explained that Ewan's money, essential to keep the business afloat, depended on marriage by her twenty-first birthday, so she had better decide to accept him and make the best of it as she had no choice in the matter.

"This isn't the Victorian age!" she had shouted at him. "You can't force me to do as you want! I won't ever marry him!"

Michael Graham's answer had been to lock her into her bedroom. It seemed incredible now, looking at him, that she could have been so naive, letting him bully her for so long. He'd treated her like a prisoner for days, bringing her up a meagre ration of food, three times a day, but refusing to let her out or even speak to her until she agreed to marry Ewan.

No one would believe such things could happen these days, Carol thought, sitting in her father's study and remembering how he had behaved. He looked older, shrunken now, less a tyrant.

"Ewan will be here later this morning,"

Michael Graham said. There was a nervous tremble in his voice. "Heaven alone knows what he'll say when he sees you like that."

"Probably he won't want to marry me any more," Carol suggested. She was amazed to see her father sag against the door. For the first time in her life she saw a defeated expression on his face.

"Claire — you have to marry him. The business — my whole livelihood depends on it. You know it was part of the bargain he and I made."

"I'm sorry, father, but you had no right to make any such bargain concerning me," Carol said. "I won't ever marry him! I detest him."

"You've changed. I don't know what's been happening to you, but you've developed a very wicked, defiant streak. I suppose you got yourself into that condition deliberately, to put Ewan off."

"No, I didn't. I told you, I was raped."

222

"Well, it won't help you. You'll have it adopted."

"No, I won't!"

"Ah!" Michael's head came up and his eyes gleamed in triumph. "If you had really been raped, my girl, you'd *want* to have it adopted. You've been sleeping around with men, haven't you, you slut!"

"No, I haven't." In spite of her new-found courage, Carol shrank back as her father came a step towards her.

"It can't be all that long before it's born," he said standing over her. "When is it due?"

"The end of September," she muttered.

Michael's face cleared. The worry went from his eyes and he said, "Only just over a couple of months. After all, Ewan needn't know. You mustn't let him see you until afterwards. No one need know you've even come back."

"I'm not going away until I've seen Ewan and told him I won't ever marry him."

"Huh! You've been saying that all

along. You'll marry him. You have to, even if it means shutting you up again for as long as it takes."

Carol knew she would not be a match against her father's strength if he decided to force her upstairs and lock her up again, though she doubted if he could carry her there now, as he had done last time. Her father's words had given her a last hope. If Ewan saw her and realised she was pregnant, whatever the cause, he most likely wouldn't consider going through with the marriage. She must see that she stayed on view until he came.

"Father, I've had a long journey over from England," she began, making herself sound docile, as if she had accepted defeat. "I haven't had breakfast. Do you think I might have something to eat? Please?"

"Bread and water's good enough for you!" he snarled. "Go into the kitchen and find some."

Thankfully, she escaped out of the room and went down the hall to the basement staircase. At least, he hadn't tried to lock her away yet.

At the top of the stair was a door, shutting off the basement from the upper floors. To her relief, she saw there was a key in the lock, and, once on the stairs, she locked the door behind her. Now she would have some warning if her father tried to come after her.

There was an outside door to the back of the house, and one that led on to the front, below the level of the pavement. She bolted the back door as an added precaution, before taking up a position by the window next to the other door, from which she had a view of the street and part of the front steps.

After some moments she heard a hammering on the door at the top of the stairs, and her father's voice shouting to her, as he realised what her plan was. Carol made a conscious effort to ignore him. Unless he contacted Ewan and told him to keep away, she shouldn't have long to wait. And if Ewan didn't come, she would go to his house and make sure he saw her.

While she stood there, resting her head against the cool glass of the window, eyes glazing with the effort of keeping watch, she marvelled how she had allowed herself to be so dominated by her father for so long. All her childhood, his word had been law in the household. She had formed the habit of doing what she was told, mainly because she had always been afraid of him and his violence towards her and her mother. But something had finally rebelled in her when she realised that marriage to Ewan would be even worse than domination by her father. When he had ranted and raged and finally locked her in her bedroom, it dawned on her that, like all bullies, he was disconcerted by defiance. That knowledge had given her the courage to take the opportunity when it eventually presented itself, and escape, taking a bag of clothes and all the money she possessed, and the ring

Ewan had presented to her, with some idea that she might sell it if she was short of funds. She had been desperate to put as much distance between herself and them as she possibly could.

The months with Luke had changed her. Never again would she allow herself to be bullied by her father. She had had a taste of what freedom and real love could be like and she would make her own future, whether or not it included Luke.

The thought of Luke made her ache with longing. The way he had walked out of the cottage two days ago — was it really only two days? — she thought in disbelief.

Her introspection was interrupted as she heard a car draw up outside. She watched, craning her neck to see up to pavement level. A man got out and ran up the steps to the front door. Carol flung open the basement door below the steps and called up to him.

"Ewan! I have to speak to you, before you go inside."

The man froze, his hand raised towards the door-knocker. He looked down over the railings and saw her.

"Claire! So you've decided to come back! What on earth did you think you were playing at? Where have you been?"

There was no sign of affection or even concern for her in his tone, only annoyance. That is my fiancé, Carol thought, with dislike. Luke, if only you knew!

"I came back to see you. I want to clear up a misunderstanding," she said.

"What are you doing down there? Open the door to me," Ewan said crossly.

When she stayed where she was, he ran down the steps and grabbed her by the arm, pulling her up with him to the front door. He hadn't changed, Carol noticed. There was still the thin, turned-down mouth, the lean, hollow-cheeked face and the black, darting, suspicious eyes. Worst of all, as he pulled her near him, she caught a

228

whiff of the halitosis which always made her heave. He was about ten years younger than her father, a dour man, utterly humourless. He had wanted a wife; Michael needed money. The deal was simple from their point of view. Neither could have hoped to acquire either easily, by any other means.

Ewan hammered on the door, still grasping Carol's arm as if he thought she would run away again. So far, he hadn't noticed her swollen belly.

Michael opened the door.

"She's come back to you, it would seem." Ewan pushed Carol inside in front of him.

"I came back for only one thing. To give you back this and tell you there's no possibility of my ever marrying you." Carol took the ring from her bag and held it out to him. Ewan ignored it. He took a good look at her and then, at last, he realised.

"What's this? What the devil have you been up to, girl?" he shouted.

"She's behaved just as I feared she

would if she ever left the protection of this house," Michael Graham replied for her. "But this needn't affect our arrangement. She'll stay here until it's over — only another few months — and then I'll arrange adoption. There'll be no more trouble. I'll keep my eye on her here and the wedding can take place quietly in October — "

"Don't you listen? Didn't you hear what I said to him?" Carol rounded on her father. "I said I'd never — "

"Be silent." Michael raised his hand and for a moment Carol thought he was going to strike her again.

Ewan burst out. "But she's pregnant! You don't expect me to marry her after this, do you?"

"Ewan — the arrangement — I'm desperate for the cash — " Michael's face turned grey.

In a rash moment of boldness, Carol held out the diamond ring to him. "Why don't you take this — Ewan doesn't seem to want it. It must be worth quite a bit."

Both men rounded on her suddenly.

"You — you gold-digging little tramp!" Ewan spluttered. "I never want to see you again! If you try getting round me — " Carol could have cheered, but her relief was shattered by a crashing blow across her cheek. "I'll teach you to run off and ruin everything. You've bankrupted me, you know that, don't you?"

She gasped, and stepped back at the force of the blow. Michael seized her arm, dragging her towards the stairs. "I'll teach you to defy me!" he shouted.

It was impossible to struggle against his greater strength. Carol felt herself dragged upwards. She fought, desperately, pounding him with her free hand.

"Ewan — help me!" she called.

"That I will not. After the way you've treated me, you deserve all you're going to get. Michael, I'll be in touch later." Ewan turned his back, striding down the long hallway and out through the door.

Michael had succeeded in forcing her

to the top of the stairs now. He reached out to open a door, ready to push her inside. Carol seized her chance to pull free, kicking him on the shins as she did so.

Whether he intended to push her or merely reached out to grab her again, she never knew, but she lurched violently, tried to save herself and, in her unwieldy state, overbalanced and pitched head over heels down the whole flight of stairs. She felt herself falling through space, then struck each tread of the stairs until she rolled to a halt at the bottom. She tried to get up, but a red haze swam in front of her eyes. Dimly she heard Ewan's voice. "Good God, man, you've killed her! Get the doctor, you bloody fool!" Then her world went black.

Carol lay in the neat hospital bed between cool sheets. She ached and felt bruised all over, but, as well as that, there was a curiously numb feeling inside her.

A nurse came to the side of the bed and bent over her. "Awake now, dear? There's someone to see you."

"No! I don't want to see anyone! Tell him to go away!" The old fears were back, sending waves of panic over her. She was so vulnerable here. Her father and Ewan could spin the hospital any yarn they chose; do with her now as they pleased.

"Carol, please let me see you. I want to talk to you."

Her heart soared at the sound of his voice, the use of that name. Incredulously, she called out, "Luke!" To the nurse, she babbled, "It's Luke — yes, it's all right! Please let him come in!"

He moved forward from behind the nurse, standing rather shyly by her bed.

"I don't believe it! How on earth did you get here? It's like a miracle. How could you possibly have known where I was? Are you sure you're real?"

"I'm real enough." Luke took her

hand in his firm grip. "You have a good friend in Laura Marshall. You have her to thank for my being here. She was worried about you and she thought I ought to know where you were. You'd mentioned who I was, and after you'd left, she telephoned my publishers in an attempt to contact me. Luckily, I was in the office at the time and spoke to her myself. I took a taxi to London Airport straight away. It's the first time I've ever used the name Gerald Williams to pull strings and secure a flight at short notice. Darling, are you sure you're all right now?"

"I'm all right in one sense," Carol said. "At last I've faced up to my past. You were right, I couldn't go on hiding for ever, pretending I didn't remember. It was all there, in the back of my memory, but I wouldn't accept it. I think I really wouldn't have let myself remember if you hadn't made me."

"It was braver of you than I ever imagined," Luke said. "I had no idea what kind of life you had led — if you can call it life."

"You mean, you knew where I lived — *how* I lived?"

"Laura said there was an envelope with a Dublin address among your things. She didn't like the idea of your coming back here after what you'd told her, so she memorised the address when she decided to telephone me. I went straight to your father's house, intending to bring you away, by force if necessary." Luke's mouth hardened into a grim line. "I learnt the truth about your life there, from him. Heavens above, Carol, how could you have let yourself be treated like that? It's positively archaic. It's like something from the Barretts of Wimpole Street. Why did you ever allow him to dominate you to that extent?"

Carol shook her head. "It was always like that. I suppose I never knew anything different. And he was my father. I was all he had, and he was a very lonely man. Besides, it wasn't that easy to leave; I had very little money of my own and I didn't know anyone who would have helped me. It was only when I realised I'd never be allowed to be free of Ewan that it became intolerable and I knew I had to run away."

"If he hadn't been an old man I'd have kicked him down the stairs like he pushed you.And as for Ewan — "

"It was an accident," Carol said. "I lost my footing." She wanted to change the subject, to stop Luke contemplating murder when he spoke of her father and Ewan.

"Do you know, my name's really Claire? Claire Graham! It sounded so odd at first."

"You'll always be Carol to me," Luke said. "And as for a surname, Legat or Graham, it won't matter either way. I intend to make you Carol Mackenzie as soon as possible."

Carol looked at him, dismay on her face. "But Luke — didn't they tell you? I've lost the baby."

"Yes, my dear. I'm so very, very

sorry." He put both arms round her, cradling her with silent sympathy.

"It happened when I fell. It started everything off but it was too early for him and he wasn't ready to live. So you don't have to marry me now. Jason's son doesn't need a father."

Luke pulled away from her, staring at her incredulously, his eyes blazing.

"Is *that* what you think? You crazy woman! I'm marrying you because I can't bear to think of the future without you. It has nothing to do with Jason, or your being pregnant. It never had. I love you, Carol. I want to marry *you.* Can't you understand that? Have Ewan and your father so influenced your ideas that you can't believe in love for its own sake?"

"Luke!" The word was a sob, as she held out her arms to him. "I know all about love. I've loved you for such a long time."

"Soon as you're fit enough, I'm taking you back to the cottage. We'll be married as soon as we can, and there'll be no more ghosts from the past to haunt us."

"Yes, please! And Luke," she clung to him. "I won't ever deceive you again. I promise. I won't have to, now you know about my father, and Ewan, and what happened to me before you found me."

Luke looked blank. Straight-faced, he said, "Who *are* these people, and what happened before I met you? I don't remember. I can't remember. I don't even *want* to remember."

Carol looked startled, then began to giggle. "All right, you win. But I really did lose my memory for a time. While I was in hospital, at the beginning, I really didn't know what had happened. And the, afterwards, it was easier to pretend."

"You were wise, little one, not to remember. Now you can forget it all again. Forget Claire Graham. Leave her behind in the past. Carol Legat is coming back home with me."

Carol nestled against him, utterly safe

and content now. "Carol Legat was a schoolgirl who grew out of her uniform," she said. "It's Carol Mackenzie to whom the future belongs."

THE END

DOCTOR NAPIER'S NURSE
Pauline Ash

When cousins Midge and Derry are entered as probationer nurses on the same day but at different hospitals they agree to exchange identities.

A GIRL LIKE JULIE
Louise Ellis

Caroline absolutely adored Hugh Barrington, but then Julie Crane came into their lives. Julie was the kind of girl who attracts men without even trying.

COUNTRY DOCTOR
Paula Lindsay

When Evan Richmond bought a practice in a remote country village he did not realise that a casual encounter would lead to the loss of his heart.

HOSPITAL BY THE LAKE
Anne Durham

Nurse Marguerite Ingleby was always ready to become personally involved with her patients, to the despair of Brian Field, the Senior Surgical Registrar, who loved her.

VALLEY OF CONFLICT
David Farrell

Isolated in a hostel in the French Alps, Ann Russell sees her fiancé being seduced by a young girl. Then comes the avalanche that imperils their lives.

NURSE'S CHOICE
Peggy Gaddis

A proposal of marriage from the incredibly handsome and wealthy Reagan was enough to upset any girl — and Brooke Martin was no exception.

CRUSADING NURSE
Jane Converse

It was handsome Dr. Corbett who opened Nurse Susan Leighton's eyes and who set her off on a lonely crusade against some powerful enemies and a shattering struggle against the man she loved.

WILD ENCHANTMENT
Christina Green

Rowan's agreeable new boss had a dream of creating a famous perfume using her precious Silverstar, but Rowan's plans were very different.

DESERT ROMANCE
Irene Ord

Sally agrees to take her sister Pam's place as La Chartreuse the dancer, but she finds out there is more to it than dyeing her hair red and looking like her sister.

THE WAYWARD HEART
Eileen Barry

Disaster-prone Katherine's nickname was "Kate Calamity", but her boss went too far with an outrageous proposal, which because of her latest disaster, she could not refuse.

FOUR WEEKS IN WINTER
Jane Donnelly

Tessa wasn't looking forward to meeting Paul Mellor again — she had made a fool of herself over him once before. But was Orme Jared's solution to her problem likely to be the right one?

SURGERY BY THE SEA
Sheila Douglas

Medical student Meg hadn't really wanted to go and work with a G.P. on the Welsh coast although the job had its compensations. But Owen Roberts was certainly not one of them!

CASTLE IN THE SUN
Cora Mayne

Emma's invalid sister, Kym, needed a warm climate, and Emma jumped at the chance of a job on a Mediterranean island. But Emma soon finds that intrigues and hazards lurk on the sunlit isle.

BEWARE OF LOVE
Kay Winchester

Carol Brampton resumes her nursing career when her family is killed in a car accident. With Dr. Patrick Farrell she begins to pick up the pieces of her life, but is bitterly hurt when insinuations are made about her to Patrick.

DARLING REBEL
Sarah Devon

When Jason Farradale's secretary met with an accident, her glamorous stand-in was quite unable to deal with one problem in particular.

ROMANTIC LEGACY
Cora Mayne

As kennelmaid to the Armstrongs, Ann Brown, had no idea that she would become the central figure in a web of mystery and intrigue.

THE RELENTLESS TIDE
Jill Murray

Steve Palmer shared Nurse Marie Blane's love of the sea and small boats. Marie's other passion was her step-brother. But when danger threatened who should she turn to — her step-brother or the man who stirred emotions in her heart?

ROMANCE IN NORWAY
Cora Mayne

Nancy Crawford hopes that her visit to Norway will help her to start life again. She certainly finds many surprises there, including unexpected happiness.

SHADOW DANCE
Margaret Way

When Carl Danning sent her to interview Richard Kauffman, Alix was far from pleased — but the assignment led her to help Richard repair the situation between him and his ex-wife.

WHITE HIBISCUS
Rosemary Pollock

"A boring English model with dubious morals," was how Count Paul Santana Demajo described Emma. But what about the Count's morals, and who is Marianne?

STARS THROUGH THE MIST
Betty Neels

Secretly in love with Gerard van Doordninck, Deborah should have been thrilled when he asked her to marry him. But he only wanted a wife for practical not romantic reasons.

TENDER TYRANT
Quenna Tilbury

Candy's 'unofficial' fiancé met with an accident, and although she didn't love him, she felt she could not leave him now. But at the hospital she met the popular Brendan Birch!

TELEVISION SWEETHEART
Eileen Barry

The heart plays curious tricks, and it seems hard that Jill Harris could not reciprocate the love of Tiernan Wilde who adored her. Instead she finds herself yearning for Roger Thurlow whose past was shrouded in mystery.

DESERT DOCTOR
Violet Winspear

Madeline felt that Morocco was a place made for love and romance, but unfortunately Doctor Victor Tourelle seemed to be unaffected by its romantic spell.

LAND OF TOMORROW
Mons Daveson

Nicola was going back to the little house on the coast near Brisbane. Would her future also contain Drew Huntley? He was certainly part of her present, whether she wanted him to be or not.

THE MAN AT KAMBALA
Kay Thorpe

Sara lived with her father at Kambala in Kenya and was accustomed to do as she pleased. She certainly didn't think much of Steve York who came to take charge in her father's absence.

ALLURE OF LOVE
Honor Vincent

Nerida Bayne took a winter sports holiday in Norway. After a case of mistaken identity, entanglements and heartache followed, but at last Nerida finds happiness.

ACCIDENT CALL
Elizabeth Harrison

When the Accident Unit at St. Mark's heard they were getting a new house surgeon they were delighted. But Tim Harrington was something of a playboy. It took a serious motorway accident to make Tim "grow up".

BITTER HOMECOMING
Jan MacLean

Kathleen had always loved Adam Deerfield as a brother, but it was not long before she realised that her sisterly feelings had changed into a woman's love.

LOVE BE WARY
Mary Raymond

The holiday of a lifetime with no complications. But of course she hadn't bargained for Ben Eliot and Eddie Ricquier, nor for the stormy emotions the two men would arouse in her.